The characters and events portrayed in this book are fictitious. Any similarity to real persons, living or dead, is coincidental and not intended by the author.

Printed in the United States of America

ISBN 978-0-578-74417-9
Library of Congress number: 2021948082

To Martha, my mother, who lived this story.

To Misty,
Hope to see you again

PROLOGUE

In the middle of World War II, a Naval officer returns home, surrounded by rumors of cowardice and abandoning the town's local war hero under fire. He finds his city awash with racial strife, German submarines offshore and the girl he loved questioning his real purpose for returning.

PALMETTOS AND SALTWATER

BY BRYAN BROOKS

A love song for a place that no longer exists, Old Fort Lauderdale.

Sandra and Bryan Brooks, Publishers
Fernandina Beach, Florida

CHAPTER ONE

January 21, 1942
Abucay, Bataan Peninsula
The Philippines

Fear pulsed through him as the Jeep raced through fields of sugarcane. Adding to his discomfort in the back seat, he was wedged among a Thompson machine gun, several containers of spare ammunition and boxes of hand grenades.

In the front seat Major Henry Johnson asked, "Navy, this guy you're looking for, what's his name?"

"Gator—I mean Vernon, Second Lieutenant Vernon Parnell, sir."

"So that's him. Got it right here on my duty sheet. Shows he's with the 57th Infantry, it's their first action."

"Thanks, Major," replied Lewis, snugging down his dirt-streaked peak cap, its metal crest denoting an officer in the United States Navy. Likewise filthy were his long-sleeved khaki shirt and trousers, not changed for days.

"Navy, did you say the two of you went through school together?"

"No, sir, just lived in the same neighborhood."

"Strange, finding each other on the other side of a world in the middle of a goddamn war."

"Strange might be one way of describing it, Major," said Lewis, wondering about the meaning of strange.

Leading two supply trucks, the Jeep descended down a dirt road through saltwater marsh that ended by an east-west running dam. Sandbagged foxholes along the dam's top overlooked fields of sugarcane beyond, purposely cut down to present a clear view of an approaching enemy. Adding to the deterrence, bundles of barbwire stretched along the dam's base. Barely thirty men in foxholes attempting to hold back the Japanese Army.

After helping Major Johnson and his men unload supplies, Lewis crept through some salt marsh up toward the foxholes. Slipping into one, he startled its occupant. "Hi, Gator." Confusion and fear registered on the man's face.

"Blackthorne? What are you doing here?"

Seeing his distress eroded a lifetime of misery Lewis had carried since childhood. "How are you, Gator?"

"You're from the Navy—how'd you get here?"

Confidence grew by the second. "Thought I'd stop by, you know, just say hello." Dimming some of that self-satisfaction was knowing he'd just placed his life in serious danger, as he watched Major Johnson and his supply caravan leaving. "Gator, heard it hits the fan at dark."

Dark came fifteen minutes later. Artillery, followed by men running across flattened fields of sugarcane. A rocket fired overhead gave Lewis his first sight of the Japanese Army. Looking down, Lewis saw this bully and demon from his childhood lying in a fetal position, whimpering. Fifteen minutes later, firing from the other foxholes had ceased. The enemy was coming over the barbwire at the base of the dam and he was alone.

CHAPTER TWO

Wednesday Evening, December 1, 1943
Fort Lauderdale, Florida

Death and dark nights always seem to find a common bond. A black Plymouth drove off the paved portion of Tenth Street onto a sandy trail and was soon swallowed by strands of thin pine mixed with live oak trees that had Spanish moss hanging from them. At the base of all this lay fields of sugar-white sand, partially covered by pine needles and sandspurs. Helping ensure the vehicle's disappearance into darkness were hammocks of palmetto bushes.

Barely two miles west, yet a world away from downtown Fort Lauderdale.

Five hundred yards into this scrubby wilderness the Plymouth stopped, its headlights staring silently into a moonless night. A large man emerged, opened the rear door and dragged out a young, thin black body. After dumping it in a sandspur-covered field he got back in. Seconds later the car turned around and left.

***

Two days later Lewis Blackthorne noticed a shadow through the frosted glass of his office door. The door opened showing a stocky, well-dressed man in his early sixties. Medium height, a balding head with an unsmiling face. A soft, well-manicured hand reached out. "I'm Dennis Lancaster from the law firm across the street in the Broward National Bank—"

"Lancaster, Lancaster, Hardwicke, Chandler and O'Hara," Lewis said, completing his sentence. Just hearing the name Lancaster meant instant pain for Blackthorne as he struggled to say, "My mom was a—"

"Martha Blackthorne, right. Your mother was Bill Hardwicke's legal secretary. We all deeply regret your mother's passing away. A tragedy." Lancaster paused, his hand still awkwardly extended. Lewis finally took the hand, grateful more words weren't needed. "You were in high school at St. Anthony with our junior partner, Jack O'Hara."

A shade under six feet, with soft blond hair, Lewis Blackthorne had been a skinny, insecure kid who developed a penchant for survival by running away to books and movies. Even his after-school job, ushering at the Sunset Theater on weekends, was an escape into a Hollywood movie.

World War II changed all that.

Words finally came. "Jack O'Hara... yeah, we graduated St. Anthony together back in '38. How's Jack these days?"

"Jack? Oh, he's fine." The man's impatient expression signaled that small talk wasn't why he was here. Blackthorne led the attorney toward his office overlooking South Andrews Avenue. Lancaster's perfunctory smile was gone, a curtain of seriousness drawn across his pudgy face.

Lewis sensed something distasteful about the man, nothing he could put his finger on. What he did see was someone not wanting to be here. "How may I be of assistance, Mr. Lancaster?"

The attorney plopped down in a chair, appearing undetermined on how to proceed. "The firm...our firm, Blackthorne...we need an investigator. But what with the war on and all, there aren't a lot of private investigators in Fort Lauderdale to choose from."

A real vote of confidence.

"We need... investigative work done. Jack O'Hara brought your name up at our firm's weekly meeting, mentioned knowing you from high school."

"Kind of Jack to remember me."

"Not exactly a lot to pick from...considering," Lancaster repeated, a haughty tone.

"I see." Lewis watched the attorney nervously staring down at his watch.

"Look—" Lancaster stopped then pointed out of the office

window onto Andrews Avenue. "It's almost five o'clock, let's discuss this over drinks. Down there, behind the bank on Las Olas is a small bar—"

"The Stag and Doe."

"Don't worry, Mr. Blackthorne, you'll be paid for your time, whether here or at the Stag and Doe."

Lewis smiled, a slight mocking tone, "Ah, yes, billable hours for your client?"

Not finding that funny, Lancaster harrumphed, "Might be easier to talk there."

"The Stag and Doe it is," Lewis agreed. "Fifteen minutes okay?" Lancaster nodded and ushered himself out.

Lewis Blackthorne's office was on the fifth floor of the Sweet Building, where South Andrews Avenue T-boned the top of East Las Olas Boulevard. Built in the 1920s, the Sweet Building stood eight stories high, the tallest building in Fort Lauderdale. Ten minutes later, he locked his office door and headed toward the elevator.

"Good evening, Lewis," the middle-aged elevator operator said, pulling back the gate.

"Good evening, Mr. Lockhart."

David Lockhart knew the Blackthorne family well as most people in town did. Lewis's father, Howard, an old cracker land lawyer had come down from Siloam, Georgia, in 1898. His father's law practice had done well during Fort Lauderdale's land boom years in the 1920s. That prosperity allowed Howard Blackthorne to build a two-story stucco home by the south side of the Himmarshee Canal on Southeast Eighth Avenue.

Then came the devastating 1926 hurricane, followed by the Great Depression when the stock market crashed in October 1929. People stopped coming, land sales stopped and new buildings stood empty. With every penny inside the Fort Lauderdale Bank and Trust. Its closing in 1928 left Howard Blackthorne penniless.

A family deep in Southern aristocracy soon discovered poverty's wretched reality. Resulting humiliation precipitated Howard Blackthorne's sudden heart attack and death. Lewis's mother,

Martha, was left struggling to pay bills and raise her son. His father's luxury white stucco two-story home on the Himmarshee Canal was soon replaced by a small wood-framed building north and east of downtown.

In an ironic twist, his father's home on the Himmarshee was now occupied by Willard Lancaster, brother of the man who just left his office.

Luckily, Martha Blackthorne's one year of college at Vanderbilt gave her employment as a legal secretary with the town's biggest law firm, Lancaster, Lancaster, Hardwicke, Chandler and O'Hara.

***

Getting off the elevator onto the first floor, Lewis glanced up at the Sweet Building's high-ceiling, narrow lobby. Outside, greeted by a warm Florida December day, he crossed Andrews Avenue and walked east on Las Olas Boulevard. Passing two white pillars and large orange awnings guarding the Broward National Bank's entrance, he approached the Stag and Doe. Before walking inside he looked across Las Olas Boulevard to check the Florida Theater's movie marquee: Irvin Berlin's musical *This Is the Army*. His father's death had caused him to withdraw even further into books and movies.

Dennis Lancaster was sitting by a small table in the back. "Tell me about yourself, Lewis."

A job interview. "Not much to tell—"

"Seems you knew our Chief Deputy Sheriff Vernon Parnell," Lancaster interrupted.

"Gator?" asked Lewis, suppressing a desire to get up and bolt out of the bar.

"Well, yes," Lancaster said, disapprovingly. "But now our chief deputy sheriff prefers being called Vernon."

"Yes, I knew...Vernon. We grew up in the same neighborhood but went to different schools."

Lancaster paused to take a breath. "Vernon went to Central. Seems you attended that...Catholic school."

"St. Anthony's, yes." Lewis detected a hint of disdain at the mention of the word Catholic.

"You two had problems?"

Lewis studied his inquisitor, again wondering whether to just leave. "Gator was a tough kid. Back then I suppose I wasn't. Strong eat the weak sort of thing."

Lancaster noted Lewis's now muscular form. "Vernon Parnell went to West Point. But you...you ran off, joined the Navy as an enlisted man?"

A question or an accusation? "That's correct."

Lancaster pressed, "Why not go to Annapolis, become a naval officer?"

A definite accusation. "My father had just died and I wasn't much of a student. Besides, no congressman would sponsor me for the Naval Academy."

"That's right, your father's passing," Lancaster conceded, "left your mother in a bad way. Martha worked for us...until her own sudden death."

"Sudden death, yes," Now Lewis's voice took on the accusatory tone.

"Your father, old Howard Blackthorne, damned good lawyer. Did you know he helped draw up the original lines to Broward County back in 1915?"

"I did, yes."

"But an enlisted man, Lewis—why not try for something better?"

Should he tell Lancaster he'd been given an officer's commission after Pearl Harbor? No, that might lead down a path Lewis didn't want to tread. Instead he offered, "We didn't have any money for college."

Lancaster nodded, accepting that, then took another tack. "Then there's the matter of both you and Vernon Parnell ending up together in the Philippines after war broke out."

More accusations? "Right again," Lewis said. "I was a part of a motor torpedo boat squadron—"

"PT boats?"

"Yes, stationed at Cavetti. After Cavetti fell, our squadron was sent to Sisiman Bay. From there I was detached to the Army to liaise, assist the Army in getting out of the Philippines...which never happened. "

"Liaison, using an enlisted man?"

Finally, he admitted it. "I'd been given a commission after Pearl Harbor."

"Interesting, didn't know you were an officer." Lancaster digested that a moment. "Gets a little murky after that. People here wonder why no one in the Philippines escaped, except you."

"Well, Gator and General MacArthur also got out." *Don't tell him your PT boat took Navy codebreakers out.*

Lancaster protested, "General MacArthur's a hero, ordered out by President Roosevelt. And our very own Vernon Parnell was wounded... a war hero. And of course everyone knows what a war hero MacArthur is."

"Is he?"

Lancaster's face distorted at that hint of sarcasm. "Yes, MacArthur's a hero, period! Then our own brave Vernon Parnell. Wounded while holding off the Japs singlehanded at Bataan. Won the Medal of Honor."

"Gator, a Medal of Honor?" Lewis mused. His thoughts rushed back to Abucay, that foxhole, that night. "Gator won the Medal of Honor?"

Lancaster got so emotional and choked up over mention of the Medal of Honor, Lewis thought the attorney might start retching. Then calm again, Lewis sensed him preparing for his final thrust.

"I'll be frank with you, Lewis, word going around is that you abandoned poor Vernon."

"I abandoned Vernon?" Lewis smirked.

"I don't think that's funny. I'm hearing now that you've been cashiered out of the Navy on a Section VIII discharge." Lancaster sat back, that satisfied look of a prosecutor after completing a successful cross-examination.

"Sounds bad, Counselor," Lewis agreed, shaking his head. "I'd heard some of that, too."

"Care to elaborate?"

The bartender walked over, putting the inquisition on hold. "Martini for me, Ted."

"A cold Budweiser please, sir," requested Lewis.

As the bartender moved away Lancaster pounced. "Abandoning Vernon Parnell? A Section VIII discharge?"

"Mr. Lancaster, you're free to believe what you wish."

"How'd you even get a private investigator's license, what with that Section VIII discharge?"

Blackthorne reached back and removed a laminated card from his wallet. "Care to check it?"

Briefly glancing at the license to conduct private investigations in the state of Florida, Lancaster asked, "What went on over there in the Philippines?"

"Guess the short answer is Gator got wounded, won the Medal of Honor and got out. And I,"—*Don't tell him why*—"was lucky enough to get away, too. Suddenly I'm here with a war still going on and, well, you know how it is, people talk."

Lancaster persisted, "What about this Section VIII?"

"It's deeply personal, Mr. Lancaster."

Lancaster paused, studying Lewis's reaction. Changing gears he said, "It seems that you and Vernon both dated my brother's daughter, Mally."

Instant pain… Gator Parnell taking Mally Lancaster to the prom. Lewis paused a moment, then said, "Mally and Vernon both went to Central, but we all lived in the same neighborhood."

"You dated the daughter of Willard Lancaster, my brother, the head of our firm?"

The asshole now living in my father's house on the Himmarshee Canal. "Yes."

"And you won't discuss the Philippines, or what happened to you in the Navy? Even if it costs you working for our law firm?"

Lewis's sad blue eyes silently acknowledged that.

Lancaster stared at his drink, a dilemma. When he looked up, Lewis knew a decision had been made. "Well, Jack O'Hara spoke highly of you. And your mother of course…we all respected her service to the firm."

Another tragedy. Lewis intended to find out just how his mother died while he was off fighting a war in the Pacific. Told it was a sudden heart attack. Found slumped over at her desk inside the offices of Lancaster, Lancaster, Hardwicke, Chandler and O'Hara. He was not even able to attend her funeral.

It was the first thing Lewis did on getting his license as a private investigator: check police and medical records.

"Well, for the firm's sake, time being the essence, I'll go with Jack's recommendation. Willard's out of town and we need to move quickly on this."

Any port in a storm—guess today I'm that port. "Mally's father is out of town?"

"Willard went to Washington, some important issues for the firm. Critical we move on this matter, now."

Interview over, time for business. "Look, Lewis, our firm has a client who owns a bar and nightclub."

"This one?"

"Well, yes, this one, too. But our client's main problem involves Club Alamo."

Club Alamo, a mystery already. "What's going on at Club Alamo?"

"A bit complicated. First off, our client's a Jew." Jew, Catholic, both words putting unpleasant expressions on Lancaster's face.

"What's his name?"

"Sam Rothstein."

***

Jew. That word triggered memories. High school, reading a brochure from the Lauderdale Beach Hotel: *"Splendid cuisine, open December to May, European or American plan. Cocktail lounge and terrace."* Then code words at the bottom of the brochure: *"Restricted Clientele."* His mother explained: "Jews, Lewis, it means Jews. Jews aren't welcome in Fort Lauderdale."

A Southern white child's question, "Jews, are they as bad as niggers, Mom?"

***

"What's your client's problem, Mr. Lancaster?"

"Won't say much, apparently someone's causing his nightclub some problems."

"Why not report it to the police?"

An awkward expression. "Seems our client doesn't want police involved."

CHAPTER THREE

Twenty minutes later Lewis Blackthorne drove his black Model A Ford down Las Olas Boulevard, away from a setting sun about to dive into the Everglades. At Third Avenue with First Baptist and St. Anthony's churches on his left, he glanced right toward Beck's Drug Store. Memories. Hours spent by the soda counter, gazing at the soft brown hair and green eyes of Mally Lancaster.

Soon, he passed the Colony Theater, then stopped for a red light at South Federal Highway. Looking left beyond Firestone Tire Store on the corner, he saw traffic backed north on Federal Highway beyond Fort Lauderdale High School two blocks away.

Looking south explained why—the Federal Highway Bridge was raised for a late returning fishing boat. By now most of the charter fleet's catch was already nailed up on display racks strung along New River. One of Fort Lauderdale's main attractions was walking along New River's sea wall each afternoon viewing the day's ocean harvest.

Still stuck at the light, Lewis's empty stomach cried seeing people go into the Bamboo Chinese Bar and Restaurant. By the base of the Federal Highway Bridge was the Pioneer House Restaurant. The restaurant initially had been a Seminole Indian trading post, set up in 1895 by Frank Stranahan.

The Seminoles had been pushed west toward the Everglades as the town grew. Though Stranahan prospered, some still remembered his horse kept for those late-night rides helping old Indian friends bury their loved ones. Eventually Stranahan became a board member of the Fort Lauderdale Bank and Trust. When Florida's land boom crashed, it closed. Devastated, Stranahan jumped into New River with a weight tied around him. His widow, Ivy

Cromartie, the town's first schoolteacher, now lived on the top floor of the Pioneer House Restaurant.

When the bridge opened and the light turned green, Lewis drove past trendy Las Olas shops and restaurants over a small concrete bridge. Land dredged up there formed mangrove wetlands with small finger islands jutting out north and south. Here, tall royal palm trees graced the grassy medium.

Las Olas then curved southeast over another concrete bridge to a small island and marina. A wooden swing bridge on the island's east side connected Fort Lauderdale to the beach. This small island and beach beyond were Lewis's favorite spots in the whole world.

***

Emerging from his car he walked across the marina's wooden docks, noting palm trees swaying from strong northwest winds on a dying December day.

"Laddie buck!" boomed out a deep voice heavy with Scottish brogue. Lewis waved back at the huge man standing in the cockpit of a forty-two-foot ketch. Hulking, the widest shoulders he'd ever seen. His sailboat, the Shetlands, had been Lewis's home since returning, a Navy stipulation.

Moments later down in the galley the Scotsman handed Lewis a cold, long-necked bottle of beer. Always abrasive, almost a command. "Where ye been, Lad?"

"Mike, who's Sam Rothstein?"

Curiosity showed on a handsome but weathered face. "You actually have a client?" A taunt.

"Yes, sort of. His lawyer, Dennis Lancaster, came to see me."

"Willard Lancaster's brother? Biggest law firm in town."

Lewis grimaced impatiently. "I know, Mike ... who's Sam Rothstein?"

"Dunna' you go gettin' so sassy, ye wee turd." After taking a hearty slash from his dripping cold beer, a loud voice reverberated against bulkheads. "Sam Rothstein's Jewish money, lad." There was almost a sneer in the tone. "Jewish money dunna' sit so well with some folks here."

"Tell me about Club Alamo?"

Munro cocked his head. "Now yer wadin' deep into the political shite. That's besides becomin' a right pain in m' arse."

Learning early on to survive his verbal abuse, Lewis learned to give it right back. "All right, so I'm a right pain in your ars—ass. When are you going to start speaking American?"

"Fook ye, wee shite."

"Please, Mike, Club Alamo, tell me about it."

Sulking, Munro gave in. "Rothstein bought Club Alamo nightclub three months ago."

"Why's it so far from downtown?"

"Club Alamo's where well-heeled people with cash go to gamble and see a strip show." A twinkle in his eye. "Maybe other things."

"What other things?"

"World's oldest profession, prostitution. And gambling. That's why Club Alamo's deep in the thicket."

"There's a war on, Mike, How many rich people can there be in South Florida now?"

"More than ye might know. Money people sneak up from Miami at night, high-rollers. Smart people know what's gonna happen after the war."

"After the war? What do you mean?"

Munro smiled at his naiveté. "Wee shite, dunna' ye know South Florida's land value will explode when the war's over."

"Land value, Mike?"

"Land, wee shite, tis all about Florida land."

***

In the 1920s during Prohibition, Mike Munro had run boatloads of Irish and Scotch whiskey from the Bahamas right past U.S. Coast Guard Base Six on the north side of the New River inlet. Most smugglers used high-speed motorboats, but the Scotsman's stealth and midnight high tides fooled the Coast Guard.

But along with that wavy red hair and sculpted face were the deep-set brown eyes laced with cruelty... the man known to old-timers as Black Mike. That red hair had faded into a wavy sea of gray, but those cruel brown eyes never lay far from the surface.

Lewis hated talk of future changes. Beer in hand, he walked up on deck, looking across Las Olas Sound, watching the last vestiges of a sun disappear behind homes that stretched along Idlewyld Drive. Wartime prohibition of streetlights meant pitch darkness would soon descend. With dampness creeping across the waters of Las Olas Sound, he returned to the galley.

"You really think land prices will escalate?"

"Bet your arse, wee shite. Now what's this Club Alamo thing?"

"There's been threats, Mike. And for some reason Lancaster's client isn't involving the police."

A questioning look. "Be careful before yer arse gets caught in somethin' ye kinna' handle."

"How?"

"We both know the Navy sent you back here for a reason, lad."

"About that, Mike, care to tell me why the Navy billeted me here on this boat, with you?"

"We both know this private detective shite's just cover. Don't fook it up."

A valid point, Lewis conceded, but since the Navy had never bothered contacting him, Munro's concern receded into the backwaters of his mind. Instead, pushed by an empty stomach, he went forward and removed his Heddon, three-piece bamboo flyrod.

"Fookin' toy," scoffed Munro. "Fly fishing, never meant for saltwater."

"Everyone says that," Lewis admitted, accepting Munro's perpetual scolding while navigating the narrow passageway out into the darkness.

Even in a night without streetlights, he could see that those earlier strong northwest winds had dissolved into a barely noticeable whisper. Walking to the south side of the wooden swing bridge connecting his island to the beach, barefoot, he waded out into brackish waters.

Emotional scars from a war, rumors he wasn't allowed to deny and still thinking about the girl. But here, salt air, brackish tidal water and moments alone, this ancient art fulfilled a need. Lewis learned early in life being alone didn't necessarily mean loneliness.

Munro did have a point, though—first attempts at fly fishing in saltwater were disasters. Everything, especially silk fly-line, deteriorated anywhere near saltwater. Then the fish he was after, snook, had razor-like gills that easily cut through thin fly-line leaders.

At Mike's suggestion, Lewis attached a hair-thin wire shock tippet at the end of the leader and found some occasional success. After stripping enough line out on back casts, he placed his fly where an incoming tide carried it toward explosions of snook, tarpon and jack crevalle voraciously attacking schools of mullet and other baitfish underneath the bridge.

A ten-pound snook pounced, a fishing thrill felt only through a fly rod's sensitivity. Minutes later and feeling at peace, Lewis grasped the snook by its prominent lower jaw and started toward Mike's galley to placate two empty stomachs.

CHAPTER FOUR

Tuesday, December 14, 1943

"Bill, I'm taking the boat out tonight, can you close up the shop today?" asked Henry Cole, owner of ABC Dry Cleaning on East Las Olas Boulevard.

"Sure, Mr. Cole."

Cole's employee, William Arthur, had recently moved here from Fort Wayne, Indiana. Doctors there suggested his four-year-old son Charlie's asthma might fare better in warmer South Florida's winters. Though Arthur owned his own business in Fort Wayne, he was waiting to make sure Florida worked out before investing in his own dry-cleaning business here.

But from the beginning, William Arthur noticed how different things were here. A first shock came in discovering Fort Lauderdale had recently lynched a colored man. When asking why, Arthur was told he'd raped a white woman. Yet no one knew who she was—or weren't telling.

It disgusted Arthur to learn that most people appeared proud, thinking the lynching was orchestrated by Broward County Sheriff Walter Parnell. Worse was listening to men brag about having attended the event.

Now this current mystery. Henry Cole's "fishing" trips at night into the ocean during the middle of a world war. Especially now that dreaded German U-boats were back sinking ships off both Florida's east and west coasts. It didn't take Arthur long to learn that each night Coast Guardsmen pulled a net across the opening to Port Everglades, keeping U-boats from parking offshore to fire torpedoes into anything inside the port.

At the start of the war, both north and south jetties of

Port Everglades had been extended. The north jetty was not only extended but deliberately curved southeasterly. This provided a protective lip, an opening for small boaters to enter the ocean. But why, Arthur wondered, would anyone go out at night into the Atlantic Ocean in the middle of this war?

CHAPTER FIVE

Makeup covered freckles he loved, and he almost didn't recognize her, standing there at the foot of his desk. Yet that tinge of bitterness was her. An angry voice interrupted his visual search. "Lewis, what's all this crazy stuff I'm hearing!"

"Guess word's gotten around," he said, his hungry eyes dancing over her face and soft brown hair. First her uncle, Dennis Lancaster, now her. That line in the movie *Casablanca*: "Of all the gin joints in all the towns in all the world, she walks into mine."

"Mally, how are you?"

"How am I? What the hell happened to you?"

"I'm back…it's a long story." Overseas wondering if he'd ever see her again.

Her eyes were doing their own dance before answering his question. "I grew up, Lewis." Finally a smile. "Seems you did too."

"We all do, Mally."

She gave him a teasing look. "How have I changed, Lewis?"

Acquired willpower from a war forced his heart to slow down. "God, it's good to see you."

"What about these stories going around town?"

"People talk, Mally."

She still seemed angry but with a wistful look, "Our teenage years seem so long ago." Before he could translate that, she blurted out, "I'm a reporter now."

"You, Mally Lancaster? Here or the Herald in Miami?"

"The Herald? You're kidding? No, I'm stuck here at the Daily News." A pause. "But I'm trying to get overseas."

"To cover the war? Good God, why?"

"To bear witness."

Bear witness?

"The war has changed everything. Women want more."

"I don't understand." Reflecting, thoughts flooding back to St. Anthony's, nuns teaching that women should be homemakers, God's work.

She read his confusion. "Yes, Lewis, more than some preordained life of marriage and babies." Resentment evolved into cold passion. "And more than just meeting man's needs."

Lewis wiped his forehead. This was Mally all right, bitterness always close to the surface.

"Here, I have to write for the society page, what passes for a so-called culture here. A load of crap."

Crap, she never talked that way before.

"But the danger? What can you write about war that's hasn't already been said?"

Floodgates of anger opened. "How about real people caught up in this? Men write about battles, new weapons or generals. What about people bombed nightly, crawling out of a subway tube hoping their homes are still there? For that matter, who writes about what war does to our own troops?"

She's right. That night in Abucay with Gator. Later, friends blown apart. Guilt at still being alive.

"And my editor here, what a pot-bellied anachronism from the past he is. Pretty obvious I only got this job because of my father." A humorless laugh. "Then their snide jokes in the pressroom discussing my body parts. Like teenage boys, makes me want to vomit. Tits and ass, men never graduate beyond that."

Tits and ass? That old chief petty officer dragging my virginity into a Manila whorehouse. Only he said it much cruder: "If they didn't have tits and a cunt, Lewis, who'd need 'em?" His face red with guilt at her honesty...and those body parts.

That bitterness, but is there something else?

"I don't belong to any man, Lewis. Father thought Wellesley was too liberal, but my scholarship and grades got me in. Eventually he was humiliated enough to pay for my tuition."

"What aren't you telling me, Mally?"

Hesitating, alert eyes searching, yearning to tell...what? The moment passed. "All Father wanted were cotillions and debutante balls. Basically go to college and get an M.R.S. degree—"

"M.R.S. degree?"

"Find a husband, silly, someone with a future in the law, Southern politics or medicine."

Lewis raised his hands in mock surrender. "We both know that never included me."

Awkward silence. "Going to Wellesley, meeting intelligent women, it changed me."

Who are you, Mally Lancaster? Past shock, moving through numb when other impulses kicked in. His blue eyes flirting, those body parts. Teenage memories, awkward attempts to fondle her breasts.

Understanding his wanting look, she smiled, victorious. Then, "Unfortunately I don't have a penis."

Saliva clogged midway in his throat killing any further desire to flirt. "Don't talk like that, Mally." Suddenly he was curious. "Are you seeing anyone?"

A trapped look. Exhaling slowly, her voice was coated with sadness. "You didn't know?"

"Know what?"

"I had been engaged to Wesley Chandler."

Engaged? A kicked-in-the-stomach moment meshed with regret soon evolving into curiosity.

"Wes is Barton Chandler's son, in my father's firm."

Mentally licking wounds, noticing bitterness draped over her. "Never knew Wes Chandler. Didn't he go to that private school for rich kids? You know, the one down around Broward General Hospital?"

"Fern Hall," she affirmed. Then she was teasing again. "Well, he is tall, and very good looking." She sighed. "Truth is, I never knew him either." She smiled. "He graduated from Harvard."

Harvard. Said to inflict pain. Deliberate. Struggling to suppress emotions, he slowly said, "I... I'm happy for you, Mally." Running off to join the Navy, disappearing into the miasma of a world war, what had he expected? *I shared milkshakes with her at Beck's Drug Store.*

"I broke off the engagement."

Lewis remembered she'd said "engaged," past tense. "Wes gambles, he's weak and drinks, I didn't know any of that. Father just pushed us together. I'm not even sure he even likes girls—"

"He's a queer?"

"Oh, please, Lewis, it's just a different lifestyle."

"But—"

"Father just wanted to keep me in his law firm."

"That M.R.S. degree you mentioned?" He watched her trying to suppress a smile. "Do you live at home?"

"No, Father and I are estranged."

Estranged? Then she blurted out, "Virginity isn't all it's cracked up to be."

"You've...you've been with..." Hurt, confused, wishing he'd been the one. Then guilt for feeling that.

Mally machine-gunned an accusation. "What's this about you and Gator in the Philippines? They're saying you abandoned him."

"I've heard that, too," he conceded.

"Then this Section VIII discharge, what's that?"

How to answer this. "Section VIII means I'm mentally unfit, maybe a coward, too. Or both." He forced a smile. "It seems you're all caught up on town gossip."

"I'm a reporter, I never accept anything without verifying it. The truth now, what really happened?"

"Do you think I'm a coward?"

"I honestly don't know what to think, Lewis, that's why I'm here."

Feeling the past slip away, accepting the stark reality of now, war teaches that. His voice was more confident. "You're kind of a mystery too, Mally. Let's just leave it at that?"

Stewing for a moment then reverting back to a flirtatious smile, almost ogling. "You've matured, easy to look at. Kind of amusing."

"Glad I can amuse you."

He sensed a reporter's questioning mind burrowing in, delicious eyes coldly analyzing. "What's the real reason you're back? I mean, a private investigator?" Mocking. "Trying to be Sam Spade?"

Immersed in this intellectual dance between them, he chose his words carefully. "Like you, I always was curious."

"Stop being so coy. After graduation you ran off and joined the Navy. Why?" The intellectual dance stopped; her eyes grew moist, the girl he'd loved since fifth grade. "I thought you'd ask me to your prom at St. Anthony's."

"You didn't seem very interested."

This confirmed what he'd always known: his knowledge of women was zero. "Not interested?"

He was fumbling forward, unsure. "Look, Gator took you to his prom over at Central."

Her eyes rolled upward. "I was a senior, desperate to get to a prom. You ran off. Vernon asked me."

"But, Gator?" Lewis smirked.

Fighting a smile, failing, finally laughing. "Okay, so he's an intellectual vacant lot." A look of yearning crossed her face.

"I wanted to ask you to the prom, Mally."

"Why didn't you?" Tears escaping, she looked embarrassed. Wiping both sides of her face smudged her makeup, and freckles emerged. *That's the face I loved.* She was vulnerable. *Women, different plumbing, fighting to survive, maybe we're really the same.*

Mally's demand drowned out his pathetic thoughts. "Lewis, what's the real reason you didn't ask me to the prom?"

Reaching for words, he sputtered, "Your dad made it pretty clear what would happen to my mother if I asked you to the prom."

"My father? What's he got to do with anything?"

"I'm Catholic. Said Mom would lose her job, be blackballed around town if I asked you to the prom."

"My father said that?"

"Dad had just died; things were bad for us. Couldn't do that to my Mom. I joined the Navy."

Her voice was barely audible. "Your mom was always so

sweet to me." Then, "But why didn't you even say goodbye?"

Tell her the Navy sent me here? No. But he wanted to. An image of Mike Munro wafted through his mind. *"Don't fook up your mission, ye wee shite." Mission, what goddamn mission? Nobody from the Navy even talks to me!*

Should he tell her that his father, Howard Blackthorne, once mentioned unethical practices going on within the Lancaster firm?

It's her father, can't say that.

Willard Lancaster, now living in the Blackthorne family's two-story stucco home on the Himmarshee Canal. His mother Martha Blackthorne, a widow living a tortured existence, drinking on weekends. An insecure kid facing the power of Willard Lancaster. At least running off to the Navy meant money coming home, but never escaping the memory of Mally Lancaster.

Tell her any of this? No.

A soft hurting cry escaped as she looked at the man he'd become. Mally got up and left, tears flooding down her face.

Welcome home, sailor. Mixed feelings of desire and anger whirled in his head like limestone and sand in a concrete mixer. More coffee. Savoring the burning black liquid, he gave Sam Rothstein's name to the Southern Bell operator over on Northeast Third Avenue.

CHAPTER SIX

At three that afternoon Blackthorne drove north on Federal Highway around the curve by the Green Star Trailer Park then east on Tenth Street. Small tourist cabins, hamburger stands and bars abounded on this street, mixed with palmetto bushes on vacant lots, as Fort Lauderdale was expanding northward from downtown.

A half-mile ahead, the street would split, its north fork becoming North Federal Highway again while Tenth Street continued to the beach. Just before the war, assisted by two bascule bridges, Tenth Street (later to be known as Sunrise Boulevard) made the city's second connection to the beach.

Blackthorne turned right off Tenth, going south on 18th Avenue. Up a slight incline past two large rock pits, he stopped by Club Alamo's front entrance. Inside, after adjusting to the darkness he spotted a man sitting by the bar.

The man waved Lewis over, ordering two fresh coffees from a prep cook in the kitchen. Nearby, employees stacked chairs for a sweep-down, preparing for the club's opening at six. Underneath a narrow high ceiling, the room appeared a dark mystery.

Then he saw the painting.

It hung on a wall behind the bar, a naked woman on a white horse, locks of black hair flowing down to partially cover one of her breasts. White skin, white horse contrasting beautifully with rich black hair. Eyes fixed on her too long, Lewis finally noticed a stage and dance floor by a dining area. Pool tables sat in the center with rows of slot machines lining both north and south walls. At the east end were craps and roulette tables.

"Sam Rothstein," the man introduced himself, sizing up the

young private investigator. Aware of his New York accent, Lewis kept glancing back to the beautiful woman on a white horse.

"I'm Lewis Blackthorne."

"Kinda grabs you by the balls, don't she, kid?"

Seeing his red face, Rothstein laughed. "Painting was here when I bought the place." Along with the New York accent, the term *entrepreneur*, maybe wheeler-dealer, stuck in Lewis's head.

Embarrassed at showing his inexperience with women, Lewis stuttered, "Your—your attorney mentioned you're being hassled by local people, not wanting police involved."

"Ever hear of the Ashley gang?"

An unexpected question. "Only what Dad told me. That they're dead, killed off back in the twenties."

"Apparently not all of them."

"I don't understand. Dad said the Ashleys were some renegade cracker family back in the Glades."

Rothstein smiled. "At least you know your Florida history. One of the Ashleys killed a Seminole Indian, stole his otter skins, then sold them in Miami. His body was found by a dredge operator back in the Glades. Working backward from the otter skins, Miami law charged Ashley with murder. Somehow he escaped and fled the state. Came back later to rob banks and run liquor from the Bahamas during Prohibition."

Lewis paused at the word Prohibition. Mike Munro's legendary career, running liquor from the Bahamas. *Did Mike know the Ashleys?* "Matter of fact, my friend was in that same occupation himself."

"Interesting friend, Lewis," mused the entrepreneur.

"Mike Munro? Yeah, interesting's a good word for Mike all right." Pulling his eyes off the naked woman he said, "But the Ashleys were ambushed, killed by the sheriff in a county north of here. They're dead."

Rothstein grimaced. "I'm new here, wouldn't know an Ashley from a rabbit turd, but I'm told that old man Ashley had sons and one of them had sons. It seems they're carrying on family tradition."

"Doing what?"

"Extorting me over the phone. They want a piece of my gambling action here at Club Alamo."

Lewis frowned in disbelief. Rothstein continued. "I told them to..." A chuckle. "Might a' said something about 'pounding sand where the sun don't shine.' Maybe I should have taken their threat more seriously."

"Why?"

"Because a week ago they killed a colored kid working for me."

"A colored kid?"

"Reuben Pinckney." Instant memories. Reuben's mother, Sylvia Pinckney, ran an employment service for colored citizens in Fort Lauderdale. Lewis's grandmother was fond of Sylvia Pinckney for reasons never explained to him.

Rothstein interrupted his thoughts. "The little shit disappeared a couple of weeks ago. Nice kid, boy never missed work. My chef here said he was a natural around food. Too bad he's colored, might have made it big in the food industry someday."

Rothstein's sad truth was replaced by a sadder smile. "Ambitious kid, enrolled in college classes, some colored college in Central Florida. Imagine, a black kid going to college in the Deep South? How crazy's that?"

Lewis nodded as Rothstein said, "Then Reuben just vanishes." He stared off wistfully. "Truth is, I sort of felt like a father toward him."

He put his head down a moment. "Ashleys told me where to find his body. I sent a man out there, and sure enough found what was left of Reuben west of town in a patch of woods—"

"Chateau Park?" Lewis interrupted.

"How'd you know about Chateau Park?"

"Used to hunt there as a kid, place has a dark history."

Giving him a curious look, Rothstein continued, "Anyway, after discovering Reuben's body I got another phone call. The Ashleys upped their price."

"Mr. Rothstein, have you ever actually seen any Ashleys?"

He paused. "No, just over the phone. People I talked to, like you, seemed surprised any Ashleys were still around. Old-timers said they were sort of a Bonnie and Clyde type of thing. You know, wild crime spree, ambushed by the law, dead."

"Your attorney said you didn't want any police involved. Why?"

"Not quite true, Lewis. I actually did call the police, that's where it all gets... complicated. The police must have passed it on to our sheriff here in Broward County because an hour later I was contacted by Sheriff Walter Parnell himself. It was Parnell who confirmed it was the Ashley gang, reincarnated so to speak."

"How's going to the police... or sheriff, complicated?"

"Because our dear Sheriff Walter Parnell is already extorting me."

That would complicate things. "What'd the sheriff say?"

"He'd go after those Ashleys all right but his 'protection' payments would increase, too. Word seems to have spread about how well my club is doing. Maybe a little too well."

"Why didn't you tell your attorney this?"

"Southern politics." Rothstein frowned. "Getting to the point I don't know who to trust down here anymore. And frankly, if I hadn't gotten to know Jack O'Hara real well from him limping into our club at night, that'd include you."

Limping, old football injury. Jack O'Hara, Irish Catholic in a Southern Baptist law firm, how'd that ever happen?

"You don't trust your own lawyer?"

"Don't know who to trust. Even to O'Hara, I only mentioned some people were causing me trouble. Nobody knows Sheriff Parnell and the Ashleys are both extorting me."

Lewis sipped his coffee. "So the sheriff wants even more money than you're already giving him. And you can't go to any state or federal people because your club's involved in an illegal gambling operation."

"That about sums it up." Lewis noticed Rothstein's skeptical look again. "You're kinda young, aren't you? What the hell do you even know about life?"

More votes of confidence. Coffee jump-started his emotions. *War, Mr. Rothstein. Killing, blowing things up. Seeing people I care about ripped apart.* Forcing calm, he said, "Maybe you'd be more comfortable with someone else, Mr. Rothstein."

"Now don't go gettin' all pissy on me, boy." He wiped his forehead. "Everything happening here, I'm not myself. If Jack O'Hara says you're okay..."

CHAPTER SEVEN

Rothstein said the sheriff came by Club Alamo for his cash pickup each Monday morning at nine sharp, even using an armored car like banks do. With that in mind, Lewis arrived early, sitting at the bar nursing his coffee when two large men walked in.

One was Mally's date to the senior prom, Gator Parnell. The other, older, a cigarette hanging from his lips. Gray eyes peered from a pockmarked face. Clyde Travis. Both had sport coats barely concealing large revolvers tucked in their waist. Size with guns. Remembering Abucay, the insecurities haunting dark closets inside Lewis's mind receded.

The club's low visibility kept Vernon Parnell from recognizing Lewis. And then he did, stopping midway across the dance floor while Travis continued on. "What's *he* doing here?

"New employee, Deputy Travis," Rothstein shakily replied. "Just going over our menu." Gator finally caught up, his face blanched white.

"New employee?" Travis harrumphed. "Them Ashley boys killed off your nigger cook, so you go out and hire some nigger-lover like Blackthorne?"

Nigger. That word, what it stood for. Lewis occasionally used it himself. Neither he nor his family ever questioned Southern culture, just accepted it...like everyone else. Did nigger-lover mean accepting people looking different as human beings? *That word nigger.*

Travis smirked. "Well, just so's you know," he pointed to Blackthorne, "your new employee ran off and left Deputy Parnell in a foxhole to die like a dog. Alone, surrounded by dead Japs,

Gator won the Medal of Honor. Your boy here got his ass kicked outta the Navy on a Section VIII."

Too frightened to answer, the club owner worked nervously at his coffee.

"Coward?" Lewis smiled, his eyes locked on Gator Parnell. The word hung suspended. "What about it, Gator?"

Travis didn't understand Parnell's tortured look. "Mind your manners, Blackthorne. Heard Gator here used to kick your ass a lot in the past."

Lewis's smile died since nothing funny was going on here. Smoke from Travis's cigarette wafted over the empty room as Lewis repeated, "Coward? Is that what you think, Gator?"

Aware that Travis was getting irritated, Gator blustered something unintelligible then spat chewing tobacco down on the nightclub's polished hardwood floor.

Travis turned to Rothstein. "Menu my ass, Jew boy, why's Blackthorne really here?" Pleased by the owner's frantic look, the bully was feeding an inner need. "Now don't go shittin' yourself, Jew boy."

Parnell found his voice. "Come on, Clyde, let's just get what we come for."

"Actually, Deputy Travis, I'm a private investigator—you're the reason I'm here."

"You hired a private eye, Jew boy, to do what?"

The nightclub owner pleaded, "It's not what you think, Deputy Travis, he's just here as a friend to help—"

"Yeah, right, just help with your fuckin' menu. You ain't gonna like where this ends up, Jew boy."

"Are you threating my client, Deputy Travis?"

Rothstein squirmed but Lewis pushed, "Tell me, Deputy Travis, why would the Ashleys kill off Sylvia Pinckney's son?"

Their expressions gave Lewis his answer. "What fuckin' concerns is them Ashleys to you?"

Lewis smiled. *Remember that night in Abucay, Gator?* Rothstein began feeling comforted by Lewis's presence.

Then Travis said, "All right, Rothstein, let's have it." Snatching the bulky envelope from his shaking hand, the deputy ripped it open. "Trying to short me again, Jew Boy?"

"What do you mean, Deputy Travis?"

"You're short! Sheriff Walter Parnell told you the cost of doin' business in Lauderdale just went up." A cruel laugh.

Travis's eyes kept returning to Lewis, predator sizing up prey. Large man, short dark hair, sunburnt pockmarked face. *Hours in the sun, a cracker boy like me.*

Rothstein took a wad of cash from his front pocket and handed it to Travis. "Don't short me again, Jew boy." He whirled around. "Come on, Gator. I'll find out what's clottin' your shit later, we got places to go."

As both men reached the club's entrance Lewis called out, "Nice seeing you again…Vernon."

***

Lewis remembered back to another bully who confronted him one day on a playground. Surrounded by his friends who were chanting, "Fight, fight, nigger and a white, come on, Lewis, beat that white." Knocked down. The class bell rang, letting Lewis slink back to class, a coward.

Fourth grade teacher Sister Mary Elise's voice was soothing, "A bully is always a coward." He never believed that. But after encountering the biggest bully of his life at Abucay, he realized Sister Mary Elise was right.

***

"You got balls, kid," said a relieved Rothstein when they were alone.

Lewis faked nonchalance. "Really?"

"What's this Section VIII coward stuff?"

"Kind of complicated, Mr. Rothstein. Something back in the war." The entrepreneur showed disbelief. "Gator the war hero thought I was dead. Finding out me here…he's not too happy about it. And, yes, rumors are spreading all over town."

"You, a coward? What really happened?"

Staring into his black coffee, Lewis wistfully said, "Like I said, Mr. Rothstein, it's complicated."

***

Early the next morning Lewis Blackthorne drove south on Andrews Avenue until it intersected two miles later with State Road 84. A right turn took him west, stopping three miles later for a red light at a lonely intersection with State Road 441. Green light, going west on a desolate two-lane road, encountering a row of Australian pines along a canal that stretched west as far as he could see. Australian pines had been planted and a canal dug out years earlier in efforts to drain the Everglades for farmland. A failed venture altering South Florida's ecosystem forever.

Fifteen miles away, State Road 84 ended when it met with US Highway 27 and a lone gas station called Andytown. Seeing the gas station reminded him of a recent article in the local paper: something about a sharp curtailment of the county's next three-month gasoline supply. That triggered a thought: *Oil is stored in Port Everglades; the Navy controls Port Everglades.*

Turning right onto US 27, facing limitless stretches of Everglades, he started north. A long, desolate journey toward the small village of Immokalee on the south shore of Lake Okeechobee.

CHAPTER EIGHT

His trip to Lake Okeechobee had been long but fruitful; more importantly it answered his questions. Arising early the next morning, Lewis hurriedly fixed his coffee, then drove across the island's wooden swing bridge on Las Olas Boulevard to the beach. Past the Beachcomber Restaurant he stopped at the beach and noticed palm trees standing still around the Las Olas Inn.

Straight ahead on the beach stood that familiar concrete lifeguard headquarters. Lewis parked, removed his shoes and walked over light brown beach sand until his bare feet touched tiny waves lapping against a quiet shore. Cold water. A quick awareness, it was December; even here the water temperature changed in winter.

Brine-coated saltwater washed over his toes as he walked south toward the Mediterranean-style stucco tower of the Casino Pool. Memories. Swimming with Mally Lancaster in the Casino Pool before rushing down its wide concrete steps over a basketball court to the beach. Then that race across beach sand to see who could dive into the ocean first. Teenagers, innocence combined with his newly discovered lust.

After the ocean's salty waves washed away pool chlorine, they'd walk south along the beach, encountering small jetties guarding the now silted-up New River Inlet. On the former inlet's north side sat the old House of Refuge, taken over by the Coast Guard during the days of Prohibition.

As kids in the 1930s, high tide sometimes meant ocean water occasionally still seeped across sand between those jetties into Las Olas Sound. Fun scampering across it, exploring what used to be an island wilderness.

But the New River Inlet was gone. A mile farther south along the shore came more jetties, the entrance to man-made Port Everglades. No scampering between these jetties. The inlet here was over thirty-five feet deep.

Lewis Blackthorn hated Port Everglades. To build it, a sliver of beach was cut out letting ocean water rush into four-foot-deep Bay Mabel, which was then dredged out destroying its mangroves. Mangroves, a nursery for saltwater life.

Officially opened in 1928, Port Everglades had introduced Fort Lauderdale to the world of overseas commerce, while the New River Inlet was allowed to silt over. Though only a child when the New River Inlet was open, he remembered high tide meant clear water downtown. Water downtown now stayed black no matter the tide.

The results were that Port Everglades and the war created the city's new economy. And that meant change. Change like fewer stands of palmetto hammocks and less clarity in the saltwater offshore. Palmettos and saltwater, Lewis's secret world. As he stood there, his sad eyes stared over the cerulean and chromatic waters of the Atlantic Ocean: *cherish your palmettos and saltwater.*

CHAPTER NINE

That word nigger. Restless, after lunch he closed the office and drove north on Andrews to Second Street. West across the Florida East Coast railroad tracks he entered Fort Lauderdale's other world.

Polite people called it colored town; many still said "nigger town." Lewis pulled over onto black dirt in front of Sylvia Pinckney's Employment Agency. A portly middle-aged colored woman ambled off her screened porch and approached his car. "Mr. Lewis."

"Nice to see you, Sylvia."

Sylvia. White people always called someone colored by their first name. No one in the South used "Mr." or "Mrs." when talking to people of color. That code again, never wanting to be called a nigger-lover. And Lewis was a son of the Old South

Sadness etched on a face no greeting smile could mask. "Sylvia, I came by to...I just heard about your son Reuben."

His name triggered tears. Without thinking Lewis embraced the old woman; he'd never actually touched a colored person before. Together they walked across dirt going for a front yard to her wood frame home, a gateway for employment to colored Fort Lauderdale.

Leaving him on her front porch, Sylvia disappeared and returned with coffee. "Doan' know what I'm a-gwana' do, Mr. Lewis. Reuben was my reason to get up each mornin'." Hearing colored slang only reinforced Lewis's deeply inculcated upbringing: Negroes are ignorant and inferior.

"Poor Reuben, just wanted to be a doctor. And you know what, Mr. Lewis?" He waited. "I worried, him always speakin' good English around white folks."

Something he didn't know. Reuben, polite and respectful, never spoke when Lewis's grandmother brought him to visit Sylvia. "Dr. Sistrunk and Dr. Mizell, dey always encouragin' him."

"I don't know those doctors." Instant shame, what he didn't know about his own city. Her knowing expression, how well she understood this.

"Now we gots us a new doctor down from Georgia, Dr. Kamau Montrose. Over on Sixth Street, Provident Hospital—"

"Provident Hospital." Lewis remembered being told that colored people finally had a hospital.

***

Lewis was seeing Sylvia Pinckney as a human being for the first time. Coming down from Georgia early in the 20th century with others of her race, she was part of the labor force building Henry Flagler's railroad down Florida's east coast.

When Fort Lauderdale's section was finished, many continued on with Flagler to extend his railroad south to Key West in 1912. But Sylvia Pinckney stayed, her employment agency bridging colored employment to white need.

Why did his grandmother, an aristocratic Southern white woman, bring him to the colored area of town to visit Sylvia Pinckney? Both were from Georgia, but racial and societal gaps between these two women were insurmountable. Visiting Sylvia Pinckney, even as a child he was aware of being treated like royalty. Years later he wondered if his grandmother saw herself as a plantation mistress visiting the slave quarters.

***

"Shor' sweet a' you coming, Mr. Lewis. Your grandmother, Miss Mary Sophia, Lord rest her soul, she'd a' been proud."

He let that sit a moment then asked, "Do you have any idea who killed your son, Sylvia?" Instant distress. "I was told it was the Ashley gang?"

Eyes had welled up but her face projected disbelief. Then a dignified resolve. "Dem Ashleys is dead."

Blackthorne nodded. "I just confirmed that myself, Sylvia. Drove over to Okeechobee to see an old schoolmate on the sheriff's department there. He said the same thing. Guess my question is: If the Ashleys are all dead, who killed your son? And why?"

Nervous eyes darted back and forth, wondering if anyone was listening. "Sheriff Walter Parnell, him and dat no-account Clyde Travis. Dey killed my Reuben."

She didn't mention Gator, the sheriff's brother.

"It was Reuben's English. Done tol' him, doan speak too well around white folks. But dat boy, he doan listen."

"The sheriff? Reuben was killed for speaking good English?"

More furtive looks, watching two colored men sitting on concrete blocks across Second Street from City Fuel Ice Plant. Every day colored men sat there, waiting for whites to come by offering odd jobs like mowing yards or moving furniture, preferring not to pay Sylvia Pinckney's percentage.

She whispered, "But dey's somethin' else."

Still thinking about colored people speaking the King's English, Lewis reached out to touch the skin of someone colored again. "What's the other reason, Sylvia?"

"We been holdin' secret meetin's, tryin' to start a Progressive Voters League chapter here and get folks registered to vote. Supreme Court's done outlawed dem white primaries."

White primaries, vote? Secret meetings? A world he never knew existed. "But, Sylvia, colored people already vote."

"But we gots no say in white Democratic primaries. No say in local representation." Something he'd never thought about. "Most times we meets wid Pastor Clarence Sims at AME Church on Fourth Street. But sometimes we meets...here in my home. Always know'd dey be some colored folks runnin' to tell the sheriff what we been doing."

Seeing his confusion, Sylvia worried she'd said too much. "Mr. Lewis, yo family been mighty fine to me, but we pays taxes, too. We needs representin'."

Pay taxes, need representation. But her slang kept reinforcing what every white child learns: Negroes are inferior. She watched him a moment, then said, "We still livin' wid da lynching."

"What lynching?"

"You was away, Mr. Lewis."

"Lynching? Why wouldn't my mother tell me about it when I came home on leave? Who got lynched? Why?"

Sylvia paused, a tired old face. "Always da same old story, Mr. Lewis. Dey say a white woman was raped."

"Who was raped?"

"Doan' nobody knows. But dey strung up dat poor boy Andre LeFleur."

A colored man with a French name?

"And Andre, he done nothin' wrong."

Sensing his proud white Southern heritage on trial, Lewis asked, "How can you be sure, Sylvia?"

"Cap'n Mike—"

"Mike Munro?" His eyes widened in astonishment. "Mike Munro?"

"Andre was workin' wid Cap'n Mike over in da Bahamas." She smiled. "Cap'n Mike, only white man I ever trust." The first real smile he'd seen today.

Still wondering why his mother never mentioned this, Lewis saw a young man entering the porch from inside Sylvia's home. Tall, lean and muscular, the darkest skin he'd ever seen. "Mr. Lewis, dis be my sister's son, Martin. Martin Tucker."

In this strong, dark presence, Lewis instinctively felt intimidated. Without standing, he turned. "Hi, Martin." Silent, a face portraying disgust. Lewis felt compelled to stand and shake the large powerful hand. No submissive smile, just unspoken contempt.

"After my Reuben," Sylvia's voice choked, "after my boy Reuben was..." Martin's powerful arms wrapped around Sylvia drawing her close. "After Reuben be killed, my sister's boy Martin come down from Georgia."

CHAPTER TEN

Again a shadow outside the frosted glass, the door opened and Dennis Lancaster walked in. No handshake this time, proceeding straight toward Blackthorne's office. "Lewis!"

"Yes, Mr. Lancaster." Suppressing a smile, Lewis followed Lancaster into his own office.

Discomfort and uncertainty showed on Lancaster's face, telling Lewis that whoever was in charge of the law firm Lancaster, Lancaster, Hardwicke, Chandler and O'Hara, it wasn't Dennis Lancaster. A stuttering, unsure voice. "My brother Willard just returned from New York. We need to talk."

"Yes, Mr. Lancaster." Lewis sensed what was coming.

"As you know, Willard wasn't consulted about your hiring —"

"So he sent you to fire me."

Refusing to admit that. he said, "He's decided...*we've all* decided, to go in another direction concerning the matter of Sam Rothstein and Club Alamo. Don't worry, though, you'll certainly be paid for your services."

Lewis teased with a smile, "Let's see, does that mean you're going to continue to let your Jewish client be extorted by Sheriff Walter Parnell?"

Lancaster's face flushed with indignity. "What? Extortion money to Sheriff Parnell? What the hell are you talking about? We never hired you to go out and—"

"Find the truth?" suggested Lewis.

"That's not what I said at all. We needed you to investigate... so we could help our client."

"Thought that's what I was doing, Mr. Lancaster. Helping

your client, you know…find the truth?"

Nervous eyes everywhere but on Blackthorne. "What truth?"

"Well, I discovered Sheriff Parnell is extorting your Jewish client Sam Rothstein over the gambling and prostitution operation he runs out there."

"Extortion! Gambling, prostitution, our client? Absurd."

"What part, the gambling and prostitution at Club Alamo or Mr. Rothstein being extorted to keep it quiet by our duly elected sheriff?"

Watching Lancaster, the word apoplectic came to mind. "There's more."

"What…more?" Lancaster's voice almost squeaked.

"I also suspect Sheriff Parnell, or one of his minions, either killed Sylvia Pinckney's son Reuben, or had someone do it."

Numb, Lancaster didn't answer. "Then something else came up. While I was away in the Navy it seems our sheriff lynched a colored man named Andre LeFleur."

More silence. Redness and discoloration on Lancaster's face and neck showed a war going on inside. Was this information he already knew; information he should have known, or information that never should have seen the light of day? Or maybe worse, information his brother Willard Lancaster deliberately kept from him? Lewis almost felt sympathetic.

Finally Lancaster found his voice, "You're saying Sheriff Walter Parnell lynched some nigger? That's libelous. Your private investigator's license could be taken away."

"There wasn't even a trial, Mr. Lancaster. What's that term you guys in the legal community throw around all the time: due process? The man was lynched without being proved guilty of anything. How do we even know a rape occurred? And where's the so-called victim?"

Lancaster's face looked like it would explode. "None of your Goddamn business."

Still curious to know who the rape victim was but seeing that answer wasn't coming, Lewis tried a different tack. "What do

Sylvia Pinckney and her son have to do with Rothstein's trouble at Club Alamo?"

"Jesus Christ, Blackthorne! It's true what they're saying around town, you're goddamn insane!"

"Sylvia Pinckney and Club Alamo," Lewis mused, "was it two birds with one stone?"

Lancaster's face twisted, looking like machinery after it's bombed.

"Let me guess, since Reuben Pinckney worked at Club Alamo, his murder sent two clear messages: Sam Rothstein needed to pay up or else, and Sylvia Pinckney better stop working with other Negro leaders around the state to start a Progressive Voters League chapter here."

Lewis turned to look down on the intersection of Andrews Avenue and Las Olas Boulevard. "Two birds with one stone, still trying to work that one out."

"Colored already vote. What are you saying?"

"They want to vote in white Democratic primaries where it really counts. Where they have some say on who represents them."

His dumbfounded look told Lewis that Lancaster was just as shocked as he had been. "Let me get this straight: you're saying Sheriff Parnell lynched that nigger, that he's extorting our client Sam Rothstein and killed Sylvia Pinckney's son? Are you now also saying that we're involved, too?"

"Two birds with one stone...maybe three birds," Lewis repeated.

Lancaster forced himself to look calm. "Can you prove any of this, Blackthorne?"

"Not yet."

"Didn't think so." Lancaster sighed in relief. "You're way over your head."

"That's surely possible, Mr. Lancaster." Seeing him like this, Lewis worried he might foul himself. "Then there's that matter of your client, a Jew owning two businesses, one making considerable profits off gambling. Doesn't sit too well, does it?"

"First off, I guarantee if we knew our client was involved in this he wouldn't be our client!"

"Because of gambling and prostitution, or because he's a Jew smart enough to game the system?"

"You're beyond libel now, Blackthorne. It's obvious why you were thrown out of the Navy."

"People do keep saying that," Lewis conceded, continuing to stare down on Andrews Avenue. "But who *was* that rape victim, Mr. Lancaster?"

"I'd be very careful if I were you, Blackthorne." Lancaster promptly got up and left.

That went well.

CHAPTER ELEVEN

Lewis noticed the tall, powerfully built man with a dark olive complexion. Mediterranean, maybe Italian. Definitely in charge, maybe maître d'. As he watched the impeccably dressed man direct activities near Club Alamo's entrance, their eyes locked momentarily but not looking for a table Lewis slid past. The man's dark eyes seemed to be burning a hole in his back.

He looked up, admiring four dimly lit chandeliers hanging from Club Alamo's long narrow ceiling. The dining area, dance floor and stage occupied one part of the building while people at the other end were gathered around either a craps game or the table with a roulette wheel. Slot machines lined both north and south walls wooing people on their eternal quest to try lady luck.

Sam Rothstein sat at the bar, dead center, watching all the action. He spotted Lewis and signaled his bartender to draft a beer for the young private investigator. Signs of worry, so different from that devil-may-care entrepreneur seen before. Was the maître d' an issue?

"What do you mean my lawyers fired you?"

Happy to know it wasn't Rothstein's idea, Lewis said, "Guess I found out too much."

Rothstein sighed. "It's about what happens when this damn war ends." Again, talk of South Florida after the war.

Near ten o'clock and between shows. A jukebox played Glenn Miller's "Moonlight Serenade" while waiters with black bow ties on starched white shirts moved quickly between tables, desperate to get drink orders in before the next show started.

Noting how well Rothstein's tailored dark suit hid his rotund frame, Lewis asked, "What happens when the war ends, Mr.

Rothstein?"

"Ever notice the skies these days? Not just Navy torpedo bombers from our base here but large bombers blocking out the sun like damn locusts."

"But that's military, Mr. Rothstein? When the war ends that's over."

"*Au contraire*, my boy. Those servicemen training here now, they're coming back, with their families."

Like Mike Munro. He protested, "Tourists come now—in winter. But summer heat, mosquitos? They'll scramble back north."

"Air conditioning, Lewis, ever hear of it? It's in some of your movie theaters downtown."

Blackthorne conceded that one reason for going to movies on hot summer afternoons was sitting in a dark, air-conditioned theater. Except of course, the Sunset Theatre, built in the 1920s; its giant fans on each side still swished the air around.

"I've got friends in that industry," Rothstein said, noticing the questioning expression. "Science, even medicine, gets improved by war. Maybe you've heard the old saying, 'It's an ill wind that blows no good'? Well, that's true. War, as despicable as it is, makes life better for the survivors. Technology is fast-forwarded, especially medicine. Even my daughter the doctor is forced to admit that."

His daughter's a doctor? That girl thought disappeared as Rothstein pressed on. "Guess what those servicemen streaming through here now will find when they go home?"

Playing along, Lewis said, "Cold weather? Dirty, crowded cities?"

"Bet your ass, Lewis. First cold winter, those ex-servicemen are scrambling back to our palm-studded paradise. Now factor in air conditioning and improved roads. Add new modern airliners already on drawing boards, and *voila*, the Florida of the future appears."

Depressed by this, Lewis couldn't help being swept up by an entrepreneurial mind at work. Rothstein smiled at his lost look and said, "Just remember this, kid, Florida land is the new gold."

Florida land is the new gold? "Everything, and I mean everything, will revolve around developing land!" The voice was emotionally charged now. "Ever hear of shopping centers?"

Too much. "Shopping centers?" Lewis's eyes escaped to the naked woman on a white horse behind the bar. *Why does everything have to change?*

Noticing Lewis's attention drawn back to the painting, Rothstein nodded. "Too bad she's not a blond. You know the old adage, opposites attract?"

Lewis's blond hair, naked woman's rich black hair...Rothstein was right. "Anyway, why are we talking about some naked chick on a horse? Let's talk business. Florida opens up after the war." He paused to smile. "That means new homes, suburbs and shopping centers."

"Suburbs, shopping centers?"

"Christ, kid, where have you been? And shopping centers signal the end of downtown America as we know it."

"But summer, heat, mosquitoes—"

A sigh. "New homes, suburbs and shopping centers here will all have air-conditioning."

The band returned, couples on the dance floor scampered back to their seats. "Mike says things like that."

"This Mike, the one you said ran liquor during Prohibition?"

"Mike Munro, yeah, we live in a sailboat off Las Olas." *Why did the Navy billet me there?* "I like Florida the way it is. From what you're saying, everything I love about Florida disappears."

"Heat, mosquitoes, lousy roads—you'd be sorry? Lewis, there's a term we in business use to describe what's going to happen here after the war."

"A term?"

"Yeah, kid, it's called progress." He put his arm around the young man's shoulder, a gesture of sympathy, "Anybody ever called you a dreamer?"

Mally Lancaster did. So much of her practicality was right next to him, only a cruder version. "I guess you're right, Mr. Rothstein, nothing ever stays the same."

Shouting erupted near the entrance on the other side of the nightclub. The maître d' had accosted a young man, tall, wafer thin, wearing glasses. Even with the noise, threats were heard across a crowded floor. The maître d's index finger pointed toward the entrance. Sheepishly, the young man retreated and left.

"What happened?"

Disinterested, Rothstein replied, "That kid's dad is a lawyer... wait a minute, his dad's a lawyer in the same firm that formerly employed you."

"But Willard Lancaster doesn't have any sons."

"No, not Willard Lancaster nor that useless fart sack of a brother, Dennis. That's Bart Chandler's boy."

Mally's former fiancé, Wesley Chandler? A schematic containing a thousand interlocking ways this man could cause problems for someone like Mally Lancaster flashed through his mind.

"Kid's got serious gambling problems."

Mally's description of a different lifestyle. "Been letting the kid slide since his dad's law firm represents me. But when you don't pay off your IOUs, those muscle boys over there will be like stink on shit."

How did I miss them? Physically intimidating, spaced around the club, swarthy, Italian-looking. Rothstein's voice boomed out, "Change is the only constant in life, Lewis. Winners get the bread, losers scramble for crumbs. But you may have stumbled onto something."

"Me? What?"

Rubbing his chin, the bar owner said, "I'm a Jew. People here don't want coming changes to benefit people like me."

Jews. Lewis had even suggested as much to Dennis Lancaster: Stop the Jew and keep colored people from voting, kill two birds with one stone, maybe three birds. Those birds and stones again.

Rothstein's voice grew sad. "Know what's it like being Jewish in America?" Lewis was too embarrassed to answer.

"My son Sidney, over there fighting the Nazis in North Africa, now in Italy. Fighting for fucking America. My Sidney can't even stay in a hotel here."

Guilt seeping through Christian pores.

"And if those Nazi bastards ever got their hands on my Sidney?" Seeing Lewis's discomfort, Rothstein changed the conversation. "Ever heard of the mob?"

"Only in gangster movies."

"And you're a private detective?" He shook his head. "Up North things like gambling, prostitution and loan are all controlled now by the wops."

"Wops?"

"With-Out-Papers. Guineas, for Christ's sake, Lewis. Fuckin' Italians."

Lewis wasn't quick enough to reply. Rothstein said, "That's what customs officials on Ellis Island called Italians and Sicilians coming over 'without identification papers.' Wops."

He whispered. "The wop mob is really a Sicilian organization reborn here in America." Wops, Guineas... Lewis was lost.

"Waves of immigrants came over to New York from Italy and Sicily around the turn of the century. Took over the rackets."

"But the police? What about police?"

"Police? Cops get paid off...and politicians who control the police. Consider it a tax, the cost of doing business.

"A tax?"

"Prohibition changed everything, Lewis—Guineas wised up, got corporate. Prohibition started organized crime in America."

"Organized crime? Incorporated? I've never heard that term...this really happens in America?" He stared at Rothstein, incredulous.

"Lewis, we live in a market economy, you're being sold something from the time you wake up in the morning."

"But—but the police..." Lewis persisted. "Our government's really that corrupt?"

"Supply and demand, son. Organized crime supplies products people can't buy on the open market." He paused. "Everything's for sale."

Lewis felt shame for being a part of the human race. "But surely the state or the federal government...the FBI," he said slowly. "They would have to be aware of this."

"Ah, now you mention the FBI. Consider this: How exactly did J. Edgar Hoover and his little band of FBI boy scouts make their reputation?"

Rothstein quickly answered his own question. "They made it fighting street crime, bank robbers like John Dillinger. Good versus evil, black and white. Bad guys go to jail, everybody's left warm and fuzzy. There's no black and white in organized crime, everything's in shades of gray."

"But why doesn't the FBI chase this organized crime?"

"To them it doesn't exist. J. Edgar Hoover keeps away from those gray areas, keeps chasing bank robbers, he's Captain America."

Seeking escape, Lewis's eyes shifted up again, almost a plea for help from naked lady on the horse. Rothstein persisted, "During Prohibition the mob supplied whisky and beer to a thirsty public, gray areas, no black and white. When Roosevelt made liquor legal again, they just reverted back to what worked before."

He pointed to the craps and roulette tables. "See those women there?"

A light went on. "Prostitutes?"

"Supplied by mob people from Miami."

"Those...girls, they work for you?"

"I get a piece of the action," he nodded. "Think product, son, a commodity. Hell, we're just suppling a market demand here. Only it's illegal."

"But you've corrupted the government."

"Hate to tell you this, Lewis, there ain't no Santa Claus...or fuckin' Easter Bunny." Conversation shifted again. "Kid, you ever been with a girl? You know, gotten laid?"

"I'm in...I was in the Navy, Mr. Rothstein."

"I wondered about that. Where'd you serve?"

"Over in the Pacific."

"Then please God tell me some old swabbie took your virgin ass into a whorehouse when your ship hit port, somewhere."

Lewis was too embarrassed now to even look at the lady on the horse. "Well, one night in Manila—"

"Manila, wait a minute! That's in the Philippines—the Japs own the Philippines. If you were there you'd either be dead or been captured. How come you're not dead or captured? Better yet, why aren't you still in the Navy?"

Nervous, struggling for an answer, he deflected, "Not everyone was killed or captured. MacArthur got out...but he wasn't the only one." *I've said too much.*

"I knew MacArthur got out...but you, other people?" Rothstein tried reconciling that a moment then let it go. "Well, at least you've been close to a pussy."

Humiliated by this, Lewis worked on his beer as Rothstein said, "Okay, let's get down to the brass tacks: Corrupting government is a necessary tax we businessmen pay to—"

"I know, I know, provide a product the public wants." Having an out-of-body experience, he still struggled with disbelief. "This organized crime thing really is in South Florida?"

"Bet your ass it's here, Florida's on the map."

"But you're being extorted by the sheriff."

"The sheriff and his idiot brother, the war hero, aren't smart enough to run something like this. No, they're controlled by the same damn New York family who took over my club." Looking stressed, Rothstein finally admitted, "I made a pact with a crime family from Pennsylvania to get my front money. Then some big guys from New York muscled in."

"Which one does the sheriff work for?"

The band started, and a line of girls came on stage. "Sheriff Parnell saw which way this was going and switched allegiance to the bigger guys."

Tired eyes looked down on the bar. "Their cut digs deep into my overhead. Now both crime families have the arm on me and I'm still paying the sheriff to keep the Ashleys off my—"

"The Ashleys are dead, Mr. Rothstein. Your Ashley money

goes straight to the sheriff."

He watched the man's expression change from depression to anger. "What's the group you got your money from say about these other people who've taken over your club?"

"Said sit tight, they'd take care of it. Trouble is, Lewis, they need to get along with those big guys in New York, too. Sometimes I worry that I might be—"

"Expendable?"

All this dance about me getting laid and a naked girl on a painting. He's perspiring like a hamster running inside a wheel going nowhere. Florida after the war, that's everything.

"Expendable?" Rothstein said, a tone of denial.

Now it was Lewis switching gears. "Tell me about this 'shopping center' you want to build."

The entrepreneur returned. "Property in front of us goes along Tenth Street. Someone named Clyde Beatty had a zoo there."

"Yeah, had to leave, Mom told me influential neighbors complained about his lions bellowing all night."

Rothstein shrugged. "The right people greasing political skids means Clyde Beatty and his pussycats are gone."

But the land was wild. Lewis didn't understand. "But you can't build out there, it's all rock pits and palmetto bushes."

"After the war those rock pits and palmettos get bulldozed so fast your head'll spin. That crap out there now—"

"Palmetto bushes, mixed in with pine and oak trees," Lewis said, reverently adding, "and white sugar sand."

"Well, guess what? All that palmettos and sugar-sand shit's gone, buried under concrete and asphalt." A mocking gesture. "Oh, don't worry, we'll sprinkle in palm trees and fancy plants to market it. Everything else? Concrete and asphalt."

Concrete and asphalt. Rothstein's right, there's no Santa Claus.

"I even have a name for my shopping center."

"A name?"

"The Gateway Shopping Center. After the war, Fort Lauderdale expands right out to it. Anybody coming south on US 1 into Fort Lauderdale, what's the first thing they see?"

"Gateway Shopping Center?"

"We'll be the 'Gateway' to Fort Lauderdale. Believe me, fifteen years from now nobody recognizes this place. My movie theater, dress shops and specialty stores, even a supermarket. Downtown? It'll look bombed out like London."

"But downtown," Lewis persisted, "that's the real Fort Lauderdale."

"Real Fort Lauderdale, my ass. Big stores in shopping centers can buy in bulk, sell cheap. Downtown America disappears..." A smirk. "Just like your palmetto bushes and sugar sand."

Run out the door, but where? Extinct palmettos, paved-over sugar sand?

Rothstein paused, another topic. "It's those two new bridges connecting Tenth Street to the beach that are the key."

Lewis couldn't connect the dots. "What about the new bridges?"

"It's the city's second connection to the beach, opens everything up. What I'm interested in is that swamp land between those two bridges."

"You'd fill in swamp and destroy mangroves?"

Rothstein ignored that. "Trick is to get my Gateway Shopping Center off the ground then quick buy up that swamp between the bridges before someone else does."

Connecting the dots, Lewis pushed further. "But I would think land on the beach itself would be better."

Rothstein gave a deep sigh. "Already taken, I've checked. Vast tracts have been bought."

"By who?"

Now he saw an entrepreneur running into limits. "My lawyer, Willard Lancaster."

Mally's father? "Did he say why he bought it?"

Concern showed. "No, and he's not too happy I found that out." Rothstein's face had a wistful look all children have before Christmas. "Tell you what I'd do with that land."

He paused for effect. "I'd turn it all into hotels with gambling casinos. Imagine, a beautiful city by Southern seas with great hotels and casinos. Gambling mecca of the world."

Gambling mecca because of two bridges? Mally's father.

"Strange, Lewis, how you ask all the right questions." The bartender was called over. Rothstein's coffee was replaced by several jiggers of scotch.

He instantly downed one, then another. Lewis saw the stress of a complicated lifestyle, eyes starting to dull. After the third shot, the club owner's stress began to ebb away. "What'll you have, son?"

Grateful that inquiries about his lack of sexual experience, or horrors concerning future destruction of palmettos and sugar sand were over, Lewis answered, "Just another Budweiser, please."

A look from the bartender, not friendly. And not the person he'd seen here before. *Connected to the maître d'? That other crime family?* The bartender moved away as Rothstein gulped down yet another scotch. Four so far.

Abruptly, Rothstein changed the conversation again. "What kind of music do you like?"

Confused by disjointed topics, Lewis said, "Big band, I guess, like everybody else."

"What do you think of Artie Shaw?"

Artie Shaw? A sip of beer. "Artie Shaw's music is great, Mr. Rothstein."

"What's your favorite song?"

Before Lewis could answer that, Rothstein blurted out, "What about 'Begin the Beguine' with Artie Shaw?"

"Overseas, must have heard it a million times."

"Did you ever listen, I mean, really just listen to Shaw play his clarinet during that song?"

"Not sure what you mean, Mr. Rothstein."

"Purest sound there is, it takes you on a journey. Melody, the beat, everything stays tight while his clarinet lifts you up on the ride of your life. Tempo slowly rises, sound stays pure, beat tight... then that crescendo. His clarinet opens up your pores, rivers of emotion flood out, you're sent screaming in the sky. Everything in you explodes. And you're right up there, Lewis, right up there in the heavens. All the while, melody, the beat, tight like virgin pussy, then you slowly drift down. When it's over you feel like you've been reborn. That's real music, son."

Rothstein escapes through scotch and Artie Shaw's music. "Guess I never really thought about it that way, Mr. Rothstein."

While Lewis sipped his beer, possible reasons the Navy sent him back here drifted through his consciousness. No contact yet and forced to live with Mike Munro—why? Then that other matter: what really happened to his mother.

The band's drums broke into his thoughts. Looking over, he watched costumes peeling off, customers howling for more. *I've never seen a striptease.*

Rothstein's personality was changing as he downed his last scotch. Belligerent, voice slurring, he said, "Who the fuck are you, Lewis Blackthorne?"

He glanced up to the naked girl on a horse. "It's complicated, Mr. Rothstein."

"I just bet it is, Lewis." A drunken laugh. "I like the way your mind works, kid. Keep asking questions."

CHAPTER TWELVE

Returning from the chaos of a world war had brought Lewis back to his Catholic upbringing. An only child desperately wanting to belong, by fifth grade he'd become an altar boy. His forever attraction to the opposite sex was a part of it, girls coming to mass would see him. Up there on the altar wearing a cassock and surplus, learning Latin helped an insecure boy push back the demons of not belonging.

Though altar boy days were long gone, Lewis stayed close to St. Anthony's by volunteering as an usher on Sundays to assist parishioners and take up Sunday collection. It was there he met fellow usher William Arthur. They'd stay after mass talking sports and fishing. One Sunday he was invited to dinner at Arthur's house. Talk of sports and fishing soon turned to Henry Cole and those night fishing trips into the Atlantic Ocean.

The Navy had never mentioned ABC Cleaners or Henry Cole's business on Las Olas Boulevard, but they did advise Lewis to keep his eyes open for talk of offshore activity at night. Especially if there was any kind of pattern. So when Bill Arthur mentioned that his boss took a boat out on the second Tuesday of each month, Lewis was listening.

***

Medical records showed Lewis's mother, Martha Blackthorne, was found unconscious at her desk. She was taken by ambulance to Broward General Hospital and pronounced dead. Ruled a heart attack, with no autopsy, her body was shipped straight to Fannin Funeral Home on Las Olas Boulevard, then interred at Evergreen Cemetery. The only witness? The person finding her at seven o'clock in the morning, Willard Lancaster.

While still employed as a private investigator by the law firm Lancaster, Lancaster, Hardwicke, Chandler and O'Hara, Lewis had asked Dennis Lancaster why his mother was working in the middle of the night. After his usual puffing up, Lancaster explained that a motion to be filed at the courthouse first thing in the morning had to be typed up.

"Then what?"

"I guess she had a heart attack during the night."

"Why no autopsy?"

Sounding nervous, Lancaster protested, "Not necessary, the physician on duty at Broward General Hospital ruled it a heart attack."

The doctor's name on the death certificate? Albert Pope, gone now, visiting family in Georgia.

***

After a month with no contact from Sam Rothstein, Lewis called Club Alamo. A heavily accented voice answered the phone. *The maître d'?* "Mr. Rothstein's not here."

"Who's running his nightclub?"

A pause. "I am. Who wants to know?"

Lewis cautiously answered, "A friend."

"Rothstein sold out." The phone hung up.

Early the next morning Lewis crossed Andrews Avenue and took an elevator to Dennis Lancaster's third floor office inside the Broward National Bank.

Splendor, scents from real wooden paneling, plush curtains and leather chairs. Visual candy, perception of power. Again the perfunctory handshake from Dennis Lancaster who remained seated behind a dark-stained wooden desk. "What is it, Blackthorne?"

"I haven't heard from Mr. Rothstein recently."

Lancaster retorted, "You're not employed by our firm anymore. Why's this any of your concern?"

"Have you heard from him?"

"It's none of your business."

"Well, have you?" Lancaster nervously moved papers

around. *He doesn't know either.*

A wary Lancaster asked, "When's the last time *you* saw him, Blackthorne?"

"Over four weeks ago at his club."

"Why are you maintaining contact with our client?"

Lewis almost laughed, this was all so predictable. "Well, it seems Mr. Rothstein didn't trust his own lawyers anymore. I called the club today and was told he'd sold out."

He saw a sudden look of concern. "Sold out?"

"You're his lawyer, wouldn't you know if he'd sold his business?"

A hammy fist slammed down. "Blackthorne, this just backs up what everyone's saying about you!"

"So you didn't know he'd sold Club Alamo...or maybe was forced out?" *He'd doesn't do well in poker. Growing up, tormented by his older brother Willard.*

"I think you should leave."

Feeling sympathetic, Lewis said, "Look, Dennis." This was the first time he had called Lancaster by his first name. "Something's going on over there, I'm not stopping until I find what happened to Mr. Rothstein."

"Get out now!" In the hallway watching him leave was the head of the firm, Willard Lancaster.

CHAPTER THIRTEEN

"Mike, tell me about Andre LeFleur."

Munro's brooding expression added a tone of caution. "Who told ye about Andre LeFleur?"

"Sylvia Pinckney."

"Sylvia Pinckney, backbone of the colored community."

"Why didn't Mom tell me about that lynching when I was home on leave?"

Mention of his mother brought a reaction. *He knew my mother?* Munro reached to the overhead cabinet and grabbed the scotch. Taking a quick slash, sadness turned to anger. "Header LeFleur, best mate ever shipped out."

"How come some colored guy has a French name?"

Contempt, another sip. "His da come from France, the lad's mother was Creole, New Orleans."

"Header? Sylvia said his name was Andre."

"When provoked, the lad bulled in headfirst. Handsome, too. Skin high-tone yellow." A pause. "Werna' rape."

"Sylvia told me you two were in the Bahamas when the rape happened."

"Aye, the lad was...women coudna' leave the lad alone... mostly white women."

This stabbed into Lewis's white Southern insecurities. "White women?"

"In droves."

"They lynched him for that?"

Munro nodded. "Police knew—they caught him with the wife of a Woodgate City Lumber supervisor—"

"Were they—"

"Buck naked in the back seat of her husband's car in Chateau Park. Want me to draw you a picture, wee shite?"

"What'd the police do?"

"Header ran, got to Sylvia's. I smuggled him onboard that night. Sheriff Parnell with that arsehole Clyde Travis showed on deck up two days later at gunpoint, took Header away."

"The sheriff lynched him?"

"Newspaper said the sheriff was ambushed by one hundred 'unknown' men when they took him to Miami for safekeeping. Couldna' been one hundred men here Parnell doesn't know!"

"So Sheriff Parnell lynched your friend Andre LeFleur."

"Aye, the sheriff with Travis and Hampy Stark—the sheriff made everyone there shoot Header to keep quiet…that's afore cuttin' pieces off him as trophies."

"Hampy Stark? But everyone in town loves fat old Hampy."

"Everyone white does, ask colored people what they think about Hampton Stark."

He'd lived with Munro's brooding, but this unleashed a rage Lewis had never seen. The Scotsman took another slash of scotch, suddenly calm. "Something I need to tell ye, lad."

The abusive language disappeared, yet another Mike Munro. "I knew yer mum, Martha."

Lewis recalled Munro's reaction when he mentioned her name before. "How did you know my mother?"

"Shoulda told ye, lad. Yer father had died—we met years later. A finer lady than Martha never breathed air."

"You…with my mother?" This was coming from nowhere. "But her letters, nothing…why?"

"We were planning to tell you."

Lewis sat back on the galley cushion. "That's a helluva shock, Mike." Thinking, reasoning, choking back emotion. "Mom was a beautiful woman. I'm glad it was you…I guess." His mind always racing forward. "Then tell me what really happened to her."

Cruel eyes, loud curses. "Your mum didna' just die, murdered Martha was." He paused. "I'm responsible."

Lewis grabbed the scotch away from Munro for a gulp of its

golden heat. "Murdered? Your fault?"

The Scotsman's head slumped. "It was that last night. Forced to work late so we had dinner at the Davis Cafeteria."

"Over by the Governor's Club Hotel?"

"Aye, tis the place," Munro said, staring off lost in a memory. "Martha loved the Spanish mackerel there."

"So what happened?"

They were deep into the new bottle. "'Twas there your mum told me about her journal. Things in it about the firm, documented for years. She'd just confronted Willard Lancaster that afternoon about it. He raged, but your mum kept her sails close to the wind and wouldna' tell him where she kept it."

"And you let her go back to work alone after that?"

"I let her...go." Lewis was stunned, watching tears flow down Munro's weather-beaten face. An injured child.

"I used my key to get into her apartment that morning. 'Twas torn apart. A woman named Helen Tindall answered at the office. Crying, something about Lancaster finding her...dead."

More scotch poured, then repeated, "Tis my fault."

"I always knew something was wrong. Mike, even that doctor, the one who signed her death certificate disappeared."

"Aye, Albert Pope. Been lookin' for wee Albert m'self."

"My mother murdered? Mike, who did it?"

"Whoever does Willard Lancaster's dirty work." The Scotsman's eyes were glazed with drunken anger.

Willard Lancaster, Mally's father. "If you think Willard Lancaster had my mother killed over her journal...I'll kill the son of a bitch."

Cold, determined eyes, a strong hand on his arm. "No, we wait. The war kinna' last forever."

"Does this have anything to do with why the Navy brought me back...why you have to wait for the war to end?"

That brooding look again. "Fook ye, wee shite."

Lewis drew back, calculating, "All right, so you have wait until the war ends, but what's in Mom's journal that got her killed?"

Munro stayed silent a moment, then muttered, "The lass wouldn't say... only something about new bridges and beach land bought for after the war."

Rothstein's vision.

***

Hung over and late getting to his office, Lewis saw the young woman by his office, her eyes inches from his steno-typed name on the frosted glass door. The word Jewish swirled around his mind, then the realization: *She's looking for me.* Except for his time in the Navy, the only Jews he knew of were from Pop Sterling's men's clothing store on Brickell Avenue.

A stunning sight. Midnight black hair barely touching the shoulder pads of her blue-belted, cinch-waist dress. *Naked girl on a horse in Club Alamo.* Lewis approached, aware cold black eyes were staring at him from a smooth angular face. And she was tall.

He had been aware of the female form since first grade when Sister Rose Germaine caught him crawling on the floor pretending to pick up crayons, in reality looking up little girls' dresses. That adventure ended badly when the nun dragged him to her desk. With his head placed inside her desk drawer, he was left to ponder his wickedness. An uncomfortable experience, but curiosity over the female form remained.

"Something I could do for you, miss?"

"I'm looking for Lewis Blackthorne?"

"I'm Lewis Blackthorne, how may I help you?" Instant shame—he'd extended his hand more to touch her than to adhere to social mores.

"We need to talk."

Finally he managed to articulate, "And you are?"

"Sarah Goldfine, Sam Rothstein's daughter."

He barely unlocked the door before she brushed past him going straight to his office. Awkward. "May I get you a cup of coffee?" Sister Mary Elise's seventh grade grammar class: "Lewis, use the words 'may I' instead of 'can I' when asking a question." *Thank you, Sister Elise.*

Lewis started his mother's old silver coffee percolator on his one metal file cabinet. Then turning on his only other personal possession, her Philco radio. "How do you take your coffee?"

"Black."

Waiting for the coffee to percolate, Lewis tried to reason out why she was here. *Her name... Goldfine...Sam Rothstein's daughter, she's married.* Two coffees in hand he entered his office, seeing she was sitting in his chair.

Too much. "Do you mind?" She moved to the foot of his desk. As Lewis sat down and stared out at the Broward Hotel across Andrews Avenue, he wondered if the hotel operated by that restricted clientele—no Jews—code.

He turned back and met her no-nonsense eyes. "I've not spoken with Abba in some time, and when my Ema told me his club's phone was slammed down on her...I took the train down to find out what's going on."

Puzzled by this terminology, he asked, "When's the last time you spoke to your father?"

"A month ago—he mentioned you. What's your connection with my father?"

Lewis slid past that. "So, you're a doctor? In New York?"

Realizing her father must have told him, she turned Lewis's question back around, "When's the last time you had contact with Abba?"

"Four weeks ago... Doctor." Lewis's coffee courage was kicking in, even managing a flirtatious smile. *She's gorgeous.* "Who or what is Abba...or Ema?"

Impatiently, she explained, "Ema and Abba mean mother and father in Hebrew. How do you know my father?"

Interrogated in my own office... again. "Well, let's see. His lawyer came in about six weeks ago, hired me to check into some problems you father was having...then I was fired."

Mid-January, 1944, South Florida was having one of its normal midwinter cold snaps when temperature plunges down to the low forties at night. Sarah was wearing a short-sleeved dress. "You're dressed for summer."

She shook her head, impatience growing. "Why did my

father's attorneys fire you?"

Gets to the point, just like Mally. "I dug a little too deep."

"What do you mean?"

"Your father's club had gambling, a strip show... among other things." Finally, he added, "He was being extorted."

"Extorted? By who?"

Is she a doctor or a prosecutor? "By the local sheriff who's controlled by New York City mob people. Your dad's attorneys either didn't know that, or weren't too happy I'd found that out. Then—"

"What are you talking about?"

"He got his start-up money from a crime family in upstate New York. Then another bigger one came in and took over his club, the same one controlling our sheriff." Her sad expression told Lewis she probably understood a lot of this.

"Where's my father?"

"Don't know, haven't been able to contact him. Frankly, Mrs. Goldfine, I'm worried."

A deep breath. "Tell me what you know."

With the caffeine gods blossoming, he sat back, "Okay, let's start at the beginning: A colored kid working in your dad's kitchen gets murdered."

Fifteen minutes later, Sarah stood up. "Take me to Chateau Park."

CHAPTER FOURTEEN

Cutting through colored town on the way to Chateau Park, Lewis glimpsed Gator Parnell and Deputy Clyde Travis leading Martin Tucker out of Sylvia Pinckney's house, handcuffed in the back. He pulled up in time to see a wailing Sylvia Pinckney come off her front porch in pursuit.

He heard Deputy's Travis's loud voice: "Your boy's involved in this Progressive Voters League crap." Then Travis lectured the colored minister next to her. "There's not going to be any Progressive Voters League here—best keep your people under control, Reverend."

"This man came down from Georgia, Deputy, he's not any part of that," the minister protested.

"You people ain't votin' in white primaries, get that through your head."

"It's the law now, Deputy Travis."

"Reverend, Roosevelt nigger law don't mean nothing in Florida."

At that point, Sylvia's nephew spotted Lewis. He lunged out but stopped as Travis violently yanked his handcuffs up. A motion meant to cause pain, but sheer willpower kept Tucker from showing it. Instead, calling out, "Thank you for all your help, 'Mr.' Blackthorne, sir."

First impressions, manner of speech, perfect English. Lewis had never heard a colored man speak that way. Travis yanked up on the handcuffs again. Pain too much—this time a muted grunt.

As before, Gator retreated at seeing Lewis, leaving an angry Travis to demand, "What are you doing in niggertown, Blackthorne?"

"Sylvia's an old family friend, Deputy Travis." He added, "I'm on my way to Chateau Park."

At that, Travis jerked open the door and pushed Tucker headfirst into the back seat. "Come on, Gator, let's git." He yelled back, "Reverend, keep your people here under control or I will."

"We're just demanding our rights as human beings," Pastor Sims responded.

Travis grabbed his crotch. "I got your fuckin' rights down here, Reverend." The door slammed; the car accelerated to the courthouse, and jail.

After seconds of silence, Lewis asked, "Sylvia, why did they take your nephew like this?"

She looked upset, wondering whether to trust anyone white. "Niggras like to keep secrets," his grandmother always said. Niggra, the accepted term proper Southern white women used instead of that other word.

Wiping tears away, Sylvia offered a formal introduction. "Mr. Lewis, dis be Pastor Clarence Sims from da AME church."

Pastor Sims cautiously nodded, intent on getting Sylvia back inside. Before going, she said, "Martin come down from Georgia, he ain't in da' Progressive Voters League." She drew a breath. "We just wants to vote like any other American." *Colored people voting like any other American?* Lewis embraced her. Touching a colored person again.

When he got back in the car, Sarah said, "Will you please tell me what just happened?" Before he could answer, another question. "Are these the same people extorting my father?"

Turning the car north on Third Avenue, he headed toward Tenth Street. "Yes to your second question, they're part of who's extorting your father. And as to your first question about what happened? Well, that colored woman's the mother of the murdered man Reuben Pinckney. Probably murdered to keep colored people here from registering to vote and from starting this thing they call a Progressive Voters League."

"I don't understand, can't they vote?"

"Not in Democratic primaries where real power and representation happen. Look, lady, you're in the South." He gave the words a sarcastic twist. "Lot of people here don't believe we lost that War Between the States." Cutting her off before she could ask another question, he said, "Let's get on over to Chateau Park before they dump Martin Tucker in county jail and find us there."

Minutes later his car drove off the pavement at the dead end of Tenth Street, onto a winding, sandy path through acres of a Fort Lauderdale yet to be paved over in the name of progress. Three hundred yards ahead they spotted turkey vultures circling.

Lewis could barely slow his car before Sarah opened the door and hit the ground running across white sugar sand. That cinched-waist dress high above attractive legs. *An athlete.* Lewis parked then followed her across a sandspur-laden field.

Two vultures perched on the carcass flew away; a persistent one, refusing to be intimidated by approaching humans, continued sharing its feast with swarms of maggots and flies crawling across something barely recognizable as a human body.

Stench replaced shock. So offensive Lewis had to cover his face just to stand next to Sarah. Undeterred, she studied the human remains before them. *A doctor, seen death before.*

No way to tell who this was, or had been. Sun, humidity and nature's scavengers had seen to that. Exposed bones still held slivers of sun-blackened and decaying flesh under shreds of a filthy white shirt, torn dark pants and a solitary shoe.

How'd she know to come here? Of course, he'd told her the site where Reuben Pinckney's body was found. While he admired her powers of deduction, she softly uttered, "It's my father."

"How do you know?" She pointed down at the solitary shoe with bits of rotted flesh and bone inside it.

"My father's shoe." Then leaving to circle outward, seconds later a yell. "Abba's other shoe." Lewis walked toward some palmetto bushes and saw a matching shoe. Like the first, this one held bones with decayed flesh. Winged scavengers fighting over a decaying body had managed to take pieces of her father's body away.

Ten minutes later Chateau Park's stillness was broken by sounds of an approaching car. Lewis and Sarah watched dirt clouds rise above the trees and shrub of Chateau Park until a vehicle emerged from the palmetto bushes and pine trees.

Deputy Sheriff Gator Parnell's black vehicle, three deputies getting out, all equally large. Caught off balance by seeing her, Deputy Sheriff Claude Travis demanded. "Blackthorne—?"

"This is my father. Why are *you* here?" Sarah cut in.

CHAPTER FIFTEEN

Sarah asked to use the phone when they returned to his office. "I need to call Jared."

"Jared?"

"My husband."

Married. In spite of all that happened today there was a boy-girl thing working inside Lewis. Pushing past that, he noticed now an air of acceptance. *Pieces of your father lying in a field, picked over by vultures and crawling maggots...*

Sarah told the operator to place a long-distance call. Moments later, "Jared, Abba's gone."

Muffled shouting over the phone, her voice choking, finally tears. "Yes, Jared, I'm sure. They've killed Abba."

***

Possible confrontation with Deputy Sheriff Clyde Travis in the wilds of Chateau Park had disappeared when Sarah Goldfine explained how she knew those remains were her father's. This prompted the deputy to head back and radio the dispatcher from their car. Twenty minutes later a black windowless wagon arrived. A brief conversation with Travis led the driver to produce a large-format Speed Graphic camera. A perfunctory show to perpetuate the myth that an actual homicide investigation might occur.

Seeing a pitiful gunny sack with a shovel to stuff the remains of her father in, Lewis had grabbed Sarah and led her back to his car. Numb, beyond resistance.

***

As Sarah slowly sipped his fresh coffee after the call, Lewis asked. "What's your husband do?"

"Jared's an assistant district attorney in Manhattan."

"Manhattan?" Sitting back, he folded his hands behind his head. "Wouldn't that mean your husband knows about these people? You know, where your father got his start-up money?"

"I remember Jared and Abba would talk about Florida after the war..." She stopped to think about that.

"What about you, Mrs. Goldfine—did your 'Abba' ever talk to you about this...Florida, after the war?"

"He was an entrepreneur, I'm a doctor. Our minds run in different ways."

"But your husband's a district attorney. How could he let your father get involved, knowing who these people are?"

Lewis sensed her worlds colliding. "I don't know, Abba and I never discussed it."

"Yeah, well, he sure discussed it with me."

She sat there, unsure. "What did he say?"

"His business sits next to land he wanted to develop before expanding east to some marsh and mangrove land between two waterways. His dream."

"Abba was always a visionary... I never listened."

Why does everyone in the world know about Florida's future except me... and her?

"Abba is..." face showing pain, "*was* a strategic thinker. It seems my husband was too."

The phone rang. Knowing it had to be her husband, Lewis passed the phone over. When the call ended Lewis sensed turmoil, and a desire to reach over...Catholic school guilt, wanting to touch such a lovely creature.

"Jared's taking the train down. He'll be here in two days."

A question crossed his mind. "Where are you staying?"

She pointed out the window.

"The Broward Hotel?" Those *restricted clientele signs* again. "Did you register in your own name?"

Flickers of anger dissolved into weariness then acceptance. "I used Sarah Wentworth." Barely audible, she murmured, "How can I even do Shiva?"

"Shiva?'

Sighing deeply, she gave him a contemptuous look. "It's Hebrew, a time set aside to grieve when a loved one is gone."

She stood up, distraught. "I'll take my father back to New York for Shiva...then return to find out who did this to him."

CHAPTER SIXTEEN

Lewis had never been inside Port Everglades before. Sent back to Fort Lauderdale by the Navy with three orders: billet with this strange Scotsman, play private detective—with a state license provided—and wait for the Navy to contact him.

Inching closer to the State Road 84 guard gate at Port Everglades, he realized that day had come. With a caveat: bring the Scotsman. Another shock hit when Munro presented his own US Navy ID card to the Shore Patrol security. *A Scottish citizen with a US Navy ID card?*

As they proceeded east toward the Navy administration buildings, Lewis asked, "How did a Scottish citizen get a Navy ID card?"

A curt deflection. "Tis a wonder they havna' dragged yer scrawny arse here sooner, the shite you started."

"Mike, how are you involved in this?"

The usual non-answer as Lewis parked by the newly built Navy headquarters inside Port Everglades. A place he deeply resented for destroying his beloved Bay Mabel.

The reality of now, looking at the starkly built administrative complex screaming military budget. Walking inside only confirmed that. Drab gray-painted walls lined with even drabber gray metal cabinets. Only two pictures adorned the walls: President Franklin Delano Roosevelt, and a perpetual frown from the Chief of Naval Operations Ernest J. King.

Two men were waiting, one a middle-aged civilian, the other tall and fit, with silver eagles attached to the collar of a starched khaki uniform, Captain Harmon Drysdale.

Ignoring Lewis, Drysdale looked at the Scotsman. "Munro,

you old sea dog, been way too long."

A rare Munro smile. "Aye, Harm, lots a' saltwater over the bow since we two bairns served in that last big show."

Last big show? Different navies, served together in World War I?

"Battle of Jutland, wasn't it, Mike?"

"Aye, Harm, it was."

Drysdale and Munro, two men remembering another time. "Damn dangerous, you old British sea dog—"

"Scottish sea dog," corrected Munro, words heavy with brogue.

"My apologies to Scotland, but as I recall your British Navy had the fight of its life off the Dogger Banks against those German battleships."

"Aye, Harm, a close-run thing.'"

Pleasantries about the past were over. Glancing at the civilian Jim Dillon from the Office of Strategic Services, Lewis knew this wasn't going to be some trip down memory lane between the Navy's commander at Port Everglades and former Scottish bootlegger Mike Munro.

Then Drysdale's eyes locked on Lewis. "Seems you've pissed off a bunch of local law enforcement, Blackthorne."

Lewis nodded, still wondering why someone from the Office of Strategic Services in Washington was here.

A smile. "Actually, Blackthorne, it's been damn good cover. Most people in town think you're just a Section VIII coward who got his ass tossed out of the Navy. Wonder how that rumor started?" A knowing chuckle between Drysdale and Munro.

You son of a bitch.

"Anyway, since our friend Mr. Dillon isn't here for local politics, let's get started." *Finally the reason I'm here.* "Thank God, that usher at St. Anthony's was a curious sort of fellow."

Lewis now knew who Drysdale's informant was, his brain swimming in an ocean of questions. An obedient nod. Then the representative from the OSS said, "Walter Mess."

"Sir?" asked Lewis.

"Walter Mess, OSS's biggest marine asset in the Pacific. After your PT boat got those code operators out of the Philippines..." Intense, his eyes questioning, Dillon said, "One of my people spotted you at the Navy's UDT facility in Fort Pierce, got you reassigned to us. You served under Walter Mess on his PT boat off the Bay of Bengal. PT 564, right?"

Mental gears tumbling, pieces fitting into place... Where were his coffee gods? A cautious Lewis said, "I did serve with Walter Mess, off Bay of Bengal."

Dillon nodded. "Rescuing all those downed fliers off the Burma, made quite a name for yourself, didn't you, Blackthorne? That expertise of yours using the Lambertsen—"

"Lambertsen Lung?"

"OSS trained you with it. Still don't know why your Navy rejected it."

Why does the OSS need a naval officer using a Lambertsen Lung off Fort Lauderdale?

"Walter Mess speaks highly of you. Said he'd drop your team offshore to swim in underwater and attach those limpet mines..." Then pointing toward Munro, Dillon continued, "Limpet mines supplied by His Majesty's British Navy, by the way."

Limpet mines, British Intelligence; OSS; Fort Lauderdale? His turn to speak. "Yes, sir, thank God Walter Mess was always out there waiting in the middle of the night." A picture was forming in Lewis's mind, but the same question: *why Fort Lauderdale?*

Interrupting his thoughts, Drysdale said, "Blackthorne, you're here for two reasons: your underwater expertise and your knowledge of the city."

"I don't understand, sir."

The man seemed to be wondering how much to say. "OSS and Navy are working together, but on the QT." Lewis stared at him, curious. "OSS is supplying the Lambertsen Lung, and British Intelligence is supplying their limpet mines."

A realization. "Mike's connected to British MI6, sir?"

Dead serious now, Drysdale said, "Mike was in the British Navy when we knew each other in World War I. Since then, MI6."

Bootlegger, MI6? Numb.

Drysdale shrugged. “Sorry about that coward stuff.” A calm glass of numb poured into a cauldron of pissed off. “And you’re probably wondering why we put you with this old sea dog Munro.”

A quick calculation. “Because Mike’s in MI6 and they supplied intelligence along with limpet mines?”

Drysdale smiled. “They told me you’re a quick study.” Leaning forward, his voice soft, he said, “There’s been a threat to Port Everglades.” Lewis nodded, silent.

“Let’s talk about Port Everglades being the deepest port south of Virginia. Important.”

“Important militarily or economically, sir?”

“Both, actually, Blackthorne. Take molasses, comes up from a British firm in Cuba, stored here in large vats. Shipped to England and turned into industrial alcohol for explosives. Sugar stored here, too, plus South American ores and other chemicals. All shipped overseas for the war.”

Drysdale kept his eyes on Lewis. “But most important of all, Blackthorne, is the oil here. Fuel for everything military. Ever wonder why?”

“Coming Allied invasion of Europe?”

Drysdale sat back, stunned. “I like the way your mind works, Blackthorne.”

The second person to tell me that. “Is our port in danger from the man who owns the dry-cleaning shop on Las Olas?”

“Jesus H. Christ, Munro! Did you tell Blackthorne that?”

“No, Harm, the lad here’s a right pain in the arse but his mind’s quick.”

Former bootlegger Mike Munro, British Navy, now MI6. “Blackthorne, everyone knows we’re going to invade Europe. What no one knows, except maybe Adolf Hitler, is how vital Port Everglades is to that invasion.”

The OSS supervisor spoke up. “We now know for sure Hitler’s threat to Port Everglades is real. Thanks to MI6’s intelligence and confirmed by your friend Bill Arthur...That’s why you’re here.”

Jumping ahead, “A threat from the owner of the dry

cleaner's shop?"

An irritated Drysdale responded, "Henry Cole, the Nazi owner of the dry cleaner's shop. Put here by the Abwehr."

"Abwehr?" Serving in the Indo-Pacific theatre of the war, Lewis never heard of a German secret intelligence organization known as Abwehr.

The Abwehr sent Henry Cole to blow up Port Everglades, and I'm here to stop it by using a Lambertsen Lung?

Three men stared in silence at Lewis with looks of expectation. Drysdale broke the silence. "Actually, Henry Cole's real name is Heinrich Koehler."

CHAPTER SEVENTEEN

Knowing now that Sheriff Walter Parnell's deputies were just bagmen for New York mobsters, Lewis followed their armored vehicle making their usual Monday pickups, thinking of Sam Rothstein's comment... a business tax.

Using tactics taught by OSS in southern Ontario, Lewis watched the armored vehicle make stops at the better hotels and bars in Fort Lauderdale. Late in the day he followed them to Northwest Fifth Avenue in colored town. *Like a paper route.*

Jammed together between Fourth and Fifth Streets sat The Windsor Club, Blue Goose, The Downbeat and Blue Note. Known by police as "the Avenue," its one block was the colored downtown. After playing big hotels in Miami Beach during the winter season, big colored bands like Count Basie, Duke Ellington and Louis Armstrong often provided free concerts for the colored community on the Avenue.

Another world, watching Gator Parnell and Clyde Travis walk in and out each saloon on the Avenue to get the sheriff's cut. The game on the Avenue was bolita. Imported from Cuba, played for pennies, gambling for poor people.

That evening, back in his office the phone rang. "Mr. Lewis?"

"Sylvia?"

Minutes later on Sylvia's front porch drinking iced tea, watching her questioning looks, "Mr. Lewis, can I trust you?"

"I hope you will, Sylvia. What is it?"

"Is you wid Sheriff Parnell and dat Clyde Travis?"

Something Lewis's father told him wafted through his mind: *Lewis, life's always easier when you just tell the Goddamn truth.* "They hate me, Sylvia."

Watching, still wondering...then believing. The plump colored woman took his hands. Touching black skin again, a Southern white boy sailing into uncharted waters. Her face acknowledging everything she'd ever thought about Lewis Blackthorne was true.

"What is it, Sylvia?"

"My sister's boy, Martin Tucker."

"What happened?"

"Still got him locked up in county jail, ain't charged wid nuthin'. It's jus' like Andre LaFleur."

The lynching again. Lewis nodded. "Sylvia, did you know Andre LeFleur had been caught with a white woman?"

White versus black. That expression, wondering again if this white man could be trusted.

Like all Southern white children, Lewis was raised with the fear of being called a "nigger-lover." They're uneducated and ignorant—that's what every child was taught. "Keep them in their place" ran headlong into the decency and intelligence sitting in front of him, Sylvia Pinckney.

***

After lunch the next day Lewis walked across Andrews Avenue into the Broward National Bank. He walked past Willard Lancaster's office on the third floor. *The man who murdered my mother. We wait, the war kinna' last forever.* Soon he was inside Jack O'Hara's office.

"You've changed, Lewis."

"People keep saying that."

"No, no," O'Hara smiled, "I mean in a good way. Seems the Navy put some meat and muscle on your bones." O'Hara seemed sad as he pointed to the cane along the wall behind his desk. That horrible football injury, a leg never recovering. Jack, limping up to St. Anthony's gym stage to get his diploma.

In high school Lewis was jealous of him. Handsome, athletic, carved Nordic face, every girl with a crush on him. Now that face seemed fleshy; his perfect body showed signs of dissipation. "My law practice is deteriorating, Lewis. I'm not even allowed to attend our weekly firm meeting. Why do I think it's because of our friendship?"

"It probably is."

"Care to enlighten me?"

They sat in a sparsely decorated office. Lewis imagined what Willard Lancaster's office looked like. "Spit it out, Lewis, what the hell's going on?"

Twenty minutes later disbelief evolved to curiosity. "You're saying your mother kept a journal implicating our firm in some kind of illegal activities? And you think Willard Lancaster had your mother murdered?"

"All I know is the night Mom confronted Lancaster about her journal she suddenly dies of a 'heart attack', and somebody tears her apartment apart looking for it...There may be more."

"You've just blown my world up, Lewis, and there's more?"

"Colored people here formed their own chapter of an organization called the Progressive Voters League. The idea is to knock out white primaries and register people to vote. Not counting my mother, I think two murders are involved in that."

"White primaries?"

Lewis laughed, "And you're the lawyer? Don't feel bad, I had no idea what the hell white primaries were either."

Seeing Jack's curious stare, Lewis continued, "If colored people can't vote in the local Democratic primaries they have no say at real representation. I'm shocked, Counselor, you didn't know that white primaries were knocked out by the Supreme Court...but it's still practiced here, enforced by our sheriff."

What complete opposites they were. Jack O'Hara excelling at every sport, Lewis a skinny left-hander in right field, barely making the team. O'Hara turned around, grabbed his cane and pushed up, limping over to stare out of his window. Junior partner, his window fronted an alley running behind the bank building. Everyone else's office fronted either East Las Olas or Andrews Avenue.

"Do me a favor, Jack?"

"A favor! My legal career's turned to shit and you want a

favor?" After an unpleasant silence came that big Jack O'Hara smile. "All right, what's your favor?"

"A colored boy, Martin Tucker. Nephew to Sylvia Pinckney, who's one of the community leaders in colored town. Tucker came down from Georgia after Sylvia's son Reuben was murdered. They think he's involved in this Progressive Voters League—he isn't—but they have him locked up on the eighth floor of the courthouse."

Jack smirked. "Lewis, lots a' colored people up on eighth floor county jailhouse. Who knows, maybe some have actually broken a law."

"Don't sound like such a white Southern boy anymore, Jack."

"You may be right," he mused. "Going to Harvard, different people...it changes your perspective." Jack sat quietly a moment then said, "I knew Willard Lancaster cast a long shadow but this, it's a little scary."

"I'd be careful, Jack."

"What are they going to do, kill some helpless guy with a cane?"

Lewis's silence came back as a loud answer. O'Hara nodded in agreement. "Okay, this colored woman's nephew, tell me about him?"

"He's not charged with anything; it's been over two weeks. Now I'm not some high-falutin' lawyer like you, but even I know about habeas corpus. Holding people in jail without charging them is kidnapping." O'Hara listened intently.

"Then that lynching a few years back, Andre La Fleur."

"Back in '38," O'Hara chimed in. "We'd just graduated from high school. You had left for the Navy and I was up north prepping for Harvard. And, yes, coming home I heard rumors about the sheriff doing it."

"Jack, do you know who the white woman was that supposedly got raped?"

"I asked Willard Lancaster once."

"What'd he say?"

"Seemed upset I asked...Wait, now you mention it, if anyone

in this town would know, it'd sure as hell be Willard Lancaster."

Lewis smiled. "I know who she is."

"The rape victim…who?"

"First off, there wasn't any rape—the other way around, actually."

"What?" O'Hara said, incredulous.

"She was a white schoolteacher, caught with Andre LeFleur in the back seat of her husband's car. Her husband's a foreman at Woodgate City Lumber."

"Maybe you are an investigator."

"Let's get back to Martin Tucker. Can you find out if he's still alive?"

"Suppose you want me to nose around here for your mom's journal, too?"

"That'd be nice."

"What's he like, this Martin Tucker? I mean, what would drive the sheriff to—"

"First off he talks better English than I do, which kind of pisses people around here off. Then, like Andre LeFleur, he has absolutely no fear of white authority. And they lynched Andre LeFleur!"

A facetious question came next. "How many colored people do you even know, Lewis?"

He looked down, embarrassed. "Okay, so I don't go to colored town a lot, but can you find out if Martin Tucker is still alive?"

Still by his window, O'Hara watched newspaper trucks move slowly through the alley picking up afternoon editions of the Fort Lauderdale Daily News. "Lewis, might be a good idea you don't come around here anymore. The likes of you…not good for what's left of my legal career."

Crushed, he got up to leave. "Stop," O'Hara laughed, "I'm kidding. I mean here in my office. Let me make some discreet inquiries into this…colored gentleman and your mother's journal. I'll call you."

As Lewis was almost out of the office, Jack said, "The story going around town says you're a coward who abandoned our local war hero, Deputy Sheriff Gator Parnell. A Section VIII discharge? Tell me that's bullshit."

"That's bullshit."

A lawyer's quick mind. "This is some kind of cover isn't it? The Navy sent you back, didn't they?"

Jack read his panicked expression. "Lewis, we're in the middle of World War II. You, all fit and handsome, suddenly turn up...don't worry, it's our little secret."

Walking down the hallway Lewis saw the door to Willard Lancaster's office come open. Sitting inside was the sheriff of Broward County, Walter Parnell.

CHAPTER EIGHTEEN

Tuesday night, February 1, 1944

The small open boat worked its way east, past the opening in the submarine net and out into the Atlantic Ocean. During the day another cold front had swept down the Florida peninsula, leaving behind strong northwest winds and a star-filled moonless sky. Northwest winds across southeast Florida means water near the shore is flat like a lake, but further out beyond protection of the land, seas rapidly build. Watching this phenomenon from the shore as a child, Lewis imagined elephants marching on the horizon. Ocean smooth near the shore, but further out elephants were marching.

As the boat cleared the jetties, Henry Cole steered north of due east. Ten minutes later, spotting a flashing light cutting through the blackness, he flashed a return signal.

Bobbing up and down out where elephants marched, a dark, lean submarine was waiting for him. Cole cut his engine letting the twenty-foot open boat glide alongside the steel killer. Three men scampered down a ladder from the submarine's tower, carefully making their way across a moving deck.

Two of them threw a line to secure Cole's craft fore and aft alongside the German U-boat. Coupled together, boat and submarine rubbed and smacked against each other in choppy seas. Another man, wearing a white peaked cap of a U-boat captain, approached Cole's boat while other crewmen on the tower acted as armed lookouts.

The captain, steadying himself, awkwardly handed over a large envelope. "Herr Koehler, your orders and instructions are inside. Meet back here next month."

"Aye, aye, Kapitan," Cole responded. As U-boat crewmen released the lines, letting his boat drift away, Henry Cole stiffly raised his right arm and saluted, "Heil Hitler!" The U-boat captain grimaced, barely returning the salute. At this stage of the war, Kapitan-Leutnant Helmut Ammon's fascination with Adolf Hitler had long since disappeared.

***

A week later Lewis and Mike Munro were back in Captain Drysdale's office inside Port Everglades. "It's on!"

"But, Captain Drysdale, how sure are you this sub's going to show up?" Lewis asked.

"More confirmation, your dry cleaner friend had already copied down papers indicating a plan against Port Everglades. That's why you're here. This time the copies Arthur made gave an exact date and time. First Tuesday in March. All in German, said it took him damn near half the night to copy but OSS translators spelled it out. Port Everglades."

Lewis thought about his friend Bill Arthur and the risk involved in doing something like this. Mentioning that, Drysdale admitted, "Bothers me too, Blackthorne, but it's war—we're all expendable."

He plunged forward. "First Tuesday next month, March 7th. Cole's orders said to be on station by 2200 hours, pick up German agents from that U-boat and transport them into Port Everglades."

"To do what, Harm?" asked Mike Munro.

"Information's compartmentalized, doesn't specify anything like blowing up the port. But it's pretty obvious they aren't sneaking Germans into Port Everglades at night to open up a tourist agency."

"How does Cole even know where to meet this submarine?"

"Latitude and longitude, all there in Cole's orders. Pretty smart fella, your friend Bill Arthur. Let's pray Cole doesn't smell a rat. Our job, *your job,* Blackthorne, will be for you and Munro to be waiting for that submarine. By the way, your equipment, it finally arrived."

"Equipment?"

"Lambertsen Lung, OSS sent it. And a limpet mine, too, thanks to Mike and MI6."

Lambertsen Lung, limpet mine? Lewis took a deep breath. "Been a while since I used one, sir. Lambertsen Lung's not like riding a bicycle. Can I try it out in a pool somewhere first, sir?"

"Already taken care of. I called Pop Levitt over at the Casino Pool. Pool closing's at four during the week so Lauderdale High's swim team can practice. Pop told the swim coach that his pool's closed next Monday for maintenance on its pumps. Just make sure on Monday that your ass is there, Blackthorne. We're only getting' one chance at this, son, don't fuck it up."

Lewis finally understood: *Lambertsen Lung, limpet mine, intercept a German U-boat. That's why I'm here in Fort Lauderdale.*

***

Two days later the phone in Blackthorne's office rang. "Well, I learned about your friend Martin Tucker."

"Where is he?"

"And I may have found your mom's journal."

Lewis's emotions were screaming. "Mom's journal? Where?"

"Helen Tindal, your mother's close friend in the firm, had it. You mom got scared after confronting Lancaster and gave it to Helen, just in case."

"Why'd Helen Tindal give it to you?"

"She's hot for my body." Silence, then a laugh. "She saw me rooting around in the library yesterday after everybody left. Took a chance and approached me."

Lewis picked up concern coming through the phone line in O'Hara's voice. "Too bad she's old enough to be my grandmother. Helen was a real looker."

"Jack, you in any danger there?"

"I'm not sure."

Heart racing, he asked, "Where's the journal?"

"Helen stashed it away, won't say where. She did tell me that the stuff in it is dynamite. The lynching, plus some land deal on the beach...then something about where money came from to build those two bridges on Tenth Street."

"Jack, where's the journal?"

"Helen said she'd bring it in tomorrow." He stopped. "Listen, I've already said way too much over the phone. I'll come by after work. Where you living these days?"

"On a sailboat tied up at Lauderdale Marina down on Las Olas, a forty-two-foot ketch called The Shetlands."

"You live on a sailboat? Is this something to do with your Navy cover?"

Silence, then a facetious answer. "It's a long and sordid story —just come by." Lewis gave O'Hara directions then hung up. Six o'clock found him standing by the small concrete bridge to the island. An hour later, darkness complete and a cool rain starting, Lewis left the bridge and started back to the sailboat, alone.

Knowing the purpose for O'Hara's visit, Munro waited down in the galley. Returning alone, the Scotsman handed him a beer then went topside into a torrential downpour. Depressed and nervous, Lewis joined him, feeling pleasure in tiny raindrops attacking his face, a need to feel pain. And feeling the boat's slight motion from waters the rippling across Las Olas Sound.

CHAPTER NINETEEN

"What the hell happened, Jack?"

"Lancaster called me in before I could leave. Wanted to know if I knew what you've been up to."

"What'd you say?"

"Lied, basically. But his eyes, Christ, there's evil there I'd never seen."

"Did Helen Tindal give you the journal?"

"That's something else, she's gone. Called me last night. Lancaster cornered her, too. She panicked and gave him some cock-and-bull story about a death in the family and took the night train to Georgia... with the journal."

Mom's apartment torn apart; they didn't find it.

Later that morning Lewis drove out to the exact spot in Chateau Park where he and Sarah Goldfine found her father's body. Some measure of peace, listening to brisk winds rustle through palmetto bushes brushing against oak and pine trees. A few steps across the field triggered childhood memories...and lessons. Walking through a sugar sand field meant legions of sandspurs soon covered your pants legs.

No matter. He was drawn here looking for answers to questions he didn't yet know enough to ask. Like coming to a seashore, still the dreamer. That quiet ended by sounds of a car moving through the foliage, Vernon Parnell, alone. Gator opened his car door and started across the field.

They hadn't been alone since Abucay in the Philippines. His stride was not so pompous anymore. Seconds later, barely feet apart, Lewis straightened up, ready.

"Been a long time, Blackthorne."

"It has."

Gator's voice was barely audible. "I'm sorry."

This coming from the bully and tormentor of his youth, "Sorry? For what?"

"First off, that crap spreading around town about you being a coward, that's a crock of shit."

Lewis moved forward. "Gator, what's your brother up to?"

The deputy stared down at the sandspurs, childhood memories for him too. "My brother? Well, for starters he and Travis have almost killed that colored boy."

"Martin Tucker? Where's he now?"

His eyes were still on the sandspurs. "Stashed inside Broward General Hospital."

A white hospital? Broward General Hospital had been conceived in 1937 when the city purchased the Granada Apartments on South Andrews Avenue. Reopened the following January as a sixty-five-bed hospital, another wing added in 1942 gave it a capacity of 120 beds.

"Where exactly in Broward General Hospital is he?" *He won't even look at me.*

"A separate place, just north of the Emergency Room. Some medical supply building on the east side."

"But what doctor would treat some colored man at Broward General?"

"Old family friend, Dr. Albert Pope."

Albert Pope, the doctor who pronounced my mother dead! "Both our families go way back to Georgia in Siloam."

On a roll, Lewis asked, "Who killed Sylvia's son?"

Letting it go, relieved, Gator finally looked up. "Clyde Travis and Hampton Stark."

"Sergeant Stark, old Hampy from the city?"

"Two of 'em, always did Walter's and Willard Lancaster's dirty work." There was more. "Just like Hampy and Travis strung up that colored man, LeFleur. That's after Travis raped and killed a colored gal. Told my brother that LeFleur did both rapes and murdered this colored girl... Lynched for nothing."

"How do you know about this other rape and murder?"

"My brother Walter, he knew Travis did it, that LeFleur never raped or killed anybody. His crime was being caught in the back seat with a white woman."

Lewis sensed Gator had more, then the words came. "Lewis, Travis and Hampy killed your mother."

Confirmation, tears coming out. *My mother! The woman Munro loved.* "How'd they do it?"

"Got the keys from Lancaster, went there late and strangled her... I'm so sorry, Lewis." Tears came from Parnell's eyes, too.

Both crying now. "Gator, what did I ever do to you as a kid for you to make my life hell?"

"Thought about that a lot lately." Lewis watched him fidget, his eyes back on the sandspurs, shame. "Shit rolls downhill. My brother was always ragging on me, I needed someone to take it out on."

"Why tell me this now?"

"Eats at you, day after day, coming home, everyone thinking you're some kind of hero...especially you being back and knowing the truth." Gator's voice broke. "It's you Mally really wanted to go to the prom with."

Now Lewis stared at the sandspurs. "Doesn't matter anymore, Gator." Wiping eyes, two little boys. "My God, look at us, up to our ass in sandspurs...funny way to start a friendship."

Not understanding the irony of sandspurs, Gator said, "Lewis, what really happened that night back in Abucay? I woke up in a hospital with everyone calling me a hero."

"From what I remember, Gator, we were surrounded, you bolted and got shot. I was alone."

"What'd you do?"

"Honestly, I was scared shitless. Fired your Thompson until its ammunition ran out. When the last two came over the sandbags I used your k-bar knife." He stopped, lost in the moment. "Must have been in shock, sitting there looking at the stars for God knows how long. Then got you to a Jeep and found a field hospital."

"Why not take the credit?"

"Who knows? Told some overworked medic I found you alone defending your position to the last man... That's me, Gator, still the fuckin' little altar boy."

"So you disappeared, leaving everyone to think I'm a hero." Lewis couldn't help but smile, hearing him admit, "I was too ashamed to say anything."

"Actually, Gator, this might be the most heroic thing you've ever done in your life...to admit that. In any case, it doesn't matter anymore."

"It does to me," Parnell said, shoulders slumping while the altar boy comforted his childhood tormentor.

CHAPTER TWENTY

The man with Sarah Goldfine was short and stocky. *Husband?* Thin strands of hair fighting a losing battle were glued to a balding head. Lewis shook the man's hand but his eyes stayed on Sarah. *Not that iceberg from New York anymore.*

Jared Goldfine appeared puffed up like a peacock. Another lawyer. Lewis excused himself, went to his front office, turned off the Philco radio then prayed at the coffee altar by his mother's percolator. *Caffeine, when all else fails.* After serving both a cup, his eyes returned to Sarah Goldfine.

Am I lonely? Lusting to touch a woman's body or just desperate to communicate with someone intelligent? All three, he conceded.

Her husband's New York accent brushed his fantasies away. "Sarah's father, what did he tell you?"

Tailored suit, cuff links...never had cuff links. Before Lewis could answer, Goldfine shot out another question, "Exactly what have you found out?" Lewis wondered how many times he'd have to repeat the same damn story.

A cautious question came next. "Did Sarah's father tell you anything about his financing ...where it came from?"

Caffeine gods settling in, Lewis shrugged, "An organized crime family up North." More concern. "Apparently from a crime family controlling criminal activities in Pennsylvania and upper New York state."

The man looked upset and incredulous. "He actually told you that?"

"He did." The lawyer was calculating his every word. "Then another bigger crime family, the one controlling our sheriff, came in and took over. It seems that Sarah's dad was caught in the middle."

Emboldened, Lewis pressed, "Why didn't you stop him?"

He saw an expression of denial. "How?"

Coffee courage in full control. "Oh, I don't know...Jared. Maybe since you're a prosecutor from the district attorney's office in New York City, you had to know how bad this was all going to end up."

Her husband was less puffed up now. "Jared, you and Abba talked about Florida all the time—you had to know where his money came from."

Goldfine looked wary, retreating. "I tried, told him to stay away from people like that."

"Did you really?" Sarah said.

"Of course I did, Sarah, what are you implying?"

"Abba was a businessman with a dream," she said. "Why did you let him deal with people like that?"

Caffeine gods raging, Lewis said, "Maybe...Jared, if you could tell us what part you played in getting her father's front money."

"What part I played?" Irritation meant he was pushing the right buttons. "Who the hell are you to ask me that?"

"Just someone trying to find who killed your wife's father. Mr. Goldfine, what exactly did *you* know?"

Face turning red, no answer.

"Jared, Lewis is just trying to find my father's killer."

She never called me Lewis before. A heart rate bump-up, noticing jealousy creasing her husband's fleshy face. "I'm not myself. Your father's... murder. I'm sorry."

"A sobering experience for all of us, Mr. Goldfine," consoled Lewis, playing marriage counselor. Mind racing, returning from war, dancing on a bubble, dancing on too many bubbles.

Jared nervously whispered to Sarah as Lewis answered the phone.

"I need to see you," the soft female voice said.

Two women, neither touchable. That old chief petty officer dragging him into a Manilla whorehouse. *If they didn't have tits and a cunt, Lewis, who'd need 'em.* Calming inner explosions, Lewis whispered, "Mally, ten minutes, your office."

Goldfine stood up and cleared his throat. "We're done here, Sarah." He hesitated, sensing debate within her.

"Lewis, we'll keep in touch." *She called me by my first name again.*

When they'd left, Lewis's compartmentalized mind kicked in. Captain Harmon Drysdale yesterday had told him to shed any civilian entanglements. It was on for Tuesday, March 7, 1944.

***

Minutes later Lewis Blackthorne crossed Andrews Avenue, aware how the sidewalks seemed full of men in military uniforms. East on Las Olas Boulevard, past the Stag and Doe, a quick look over to the Florida Theater. Reaching the Blount Building at Southeast First Avenue, noticing the usual congestion by the Governor's Club Hotel.

Before turning the corner he looked cattycorner across Las Olas to what used to be the Pioneer Department Store. Taken over by the city council and business leaders after the war started, it was turned into a huge recreation center for the military personnel stationed here. In desperate need of female companionship, Lewis had contemplated going there until reminded by Mike Munro that he'd been thrown out of the Navy and was disgraced.

North of the Blount Building, Mally Lancaster waited in front of her office. "So many military people." Nervous, offering small talk. Her pinned-up brown hair reminded him of a portrait he'd seen of Ivy Cromartie Stranahan, the town's first schoolteacher and wife of Frank, the town's acknowledged founder.

Pinned-up hair seemed perfect on Mally, along with her pale white blouse and brown pleated skirt. Glancing down, he saw brown pumps. Not black-and-white saddle shoes and bobby socks that every girl wore in high school wore. "Can't talk here, Lewis." Green eyes were dancing with fire; she'd been crying.

"What is it?"

"Not here, let's get lunch over at the Maryland Hotel." Together, walking north then into the Tropical Arcade past small shops, they exited back onto Andrews Avenue. Now military uniforms were mixed in with office workers out for lunch.

Cars, people everywhere. Was it because the war was going well, or a precursor to what Florida would become after the war? Or both? Dodging cars they crossed Andrews Avenue and found a quiet table in the Maryland Hotel.

"What's so important?"

"My editor finally assigned me a story...something no one else wanted."

"What kind of story?"

"An anonymous tip, some colored man held at county jail, not charged—"

"Martin Tucker."

Her eyes widened. "How do you know about that?"

Shackles were falling from an insecure teenage boy. "Mally, just tell me, what did you find out?"

She looked a little miffed, then said, "I found the source, Sylvia Pinckney."

She is a good reporter. "I know where he is."

That verified what Gator told me in Chateau Park. Then a shock.

"I'm leaving on the train tonight. The Associated Press is sending me to cover the war in Italy."

CHAPTER TWENTY-ONE

That night Lewis saw the face of a stone-cold killer when he explained to Munro where his mother's journal ended up. Only when mentioning his plan to free Martin Tucker from Broward General Hospital did that intensity evolve into something like curiosity. "I'll be going with ye."

"Mike, you don't have to do this."

"Yer mum, Martha," he hissed, "the lass I loved." No room for debate. Lewis did have to admit having Munro involved was good, on so many levels.

A few swallows of scotch later, he said, "Isna' a trap?"

"Two sources, Mike. Two sources."

"Yer second source?"

"Mally Lancaster."

Seeing him sneer, Lewis said, "We dated in high school. Mally's a reporter."

"That's fookin' rich, the daughter of Willard Lancaster!" Then crudeness. "No, ye dunna' pick any split-tail. No, ye pick Willard Lancaster's daughter."

Hearing Mally's genitalia described like this made him scowl. "Don't say that, Mike."

Mike waved him off. "Tell me about this 'daughter' of Willard Lancaster."

"Mally's editor gave her something to run down, Martin Tucker. A colored man held by the sheriff without being charged with anything. Gator told me where he was; she confirmed it. She even found Sylvia."

"Smart lass." Then he grew suspicious. "Why are they keeping him alive?"

"They think he's involved with the colored Progressive Voters League."

"This lass, yer split-tail—"

Anger burned in Lewis, yet he remembered that night in a Manila whorehouse. Descriptions of women that he'd never objected to, on some level enjoyed.

After another swallow of scotch, the Scotsman said, "We'll need help from Sylvia Pinckney."

CHAPTER TWENTY-TWO

February 29, 1944

Early that morning three men drove up a ramp to Broward General Hospital's medical supply building: Lewis, Mike Munro and a young colored doctor from Provident Hospital, Dr. Kamau Montrose.

The young doctor followed them up a concrete ramp, stopping by two doors where trucks offloaded medical supplies. Wartime restrictions on streetlights, plus foliage from two giant banyan trees, kept both ramp and car in darkness.

With tools and a flashlight, Munro knelt by the door lock. Seconds later it opened and they disappeared, walking through several darkened aisles to the office. Dr. Montrose knelt by the mattress in the office and opened his small medical bag.

Tucker woke up, in fright then anger. "Who are you?"

"Hush, I am here to help you, Martin," whispered Dr. Montrose, his first words spoken since leaving Sylvia's house. "You are with friends now. Stay quiet, son, we are here to help."

Educated, speaks perfect English.

Munro's flashlight showed swollen eyes peering out from bandages, a mummy-like appearance. The mummy's left leg and arm were handcuffed to two newly installed metal poles.

Proper sentences, well-pronounced words, the second colored man he'd ever heard speak like this was lying on the mattress before him. Tucker eyed the colored doctor. "Who are *you*?"

"I am Dr. Kamau Montrose. Please be quiet."

Tucker glared at Lewis. "Coming to lynch me, cracker boy?" Energized by anger, he used his unshackled arm to prop up. Sharp pain, collapsing back on the mattress.

Dr. Montrose pulled up Tucker's hospital gown and started probing welts and discolored skin around ribs from the beatings; his physical appearance spoke volumes. "They're not here to lynch you, Martin," assured Dr. Montrose.

Beyond Lewis and Dr. Montrose, a huge shadow, Mike Munro. His deep voice was coated with Scottish brogue. "How much longer, Doctor?"

"Mr. Tucker has a concussion, at least one broken arm and maybe some internal injuries. This may take some time."

"We dunna' have more time, Doctor." Munro stalked out with Lewis in tow to check out the building they'd just broken into.

Noise. Light streaked through a door connecting the medical supply room to the hospital as Lewis and Munro ducked behind boxes of medical supplies. The huge hand of Sergeant Hampton Stark reached in to turn on the light.

"Well, well, what we got us here?" His gun pointed toward Dr. Montrose still by Tucker's mattress. "What are you doing here, boy?"

The colored doctor stood up and calmly replied, "My name is Dr. Kamau Montrose and I am here to treat this man."

His prey captured, Stark mocked, "Jus' what kinda' nigger name is Kamau?"

Dr. Montrose's eyes never betrayed Mike Munro's stealthy approach from behind the police sergeant, nor flinched as his blackjack split open Hampton Stark's skull.

Gushing blood mixed with boxes tumbling then a crashing thump. Contact with the wooden floor sent Stark's gun spinning back toward the large double doors they had just entered. A pool of blood from the man's cracked skull began spreading over the floor.

The face of a killer. Munro calmly spat down on the four hundred pounds of death, "This is fer Martha and Andre LeFleur, ye piece of shite." Lewis was in shock, his eyes silently pleading:

What now?

No answer came back from Munro.

Doctor Montrose walked over and glanced down, his voice soft answering the policeman's hurtful question, "The name Kamau means quiet warrior, Sergeant."

Again that cultured, another educated voice from someone in a black skin.

As Munro checked the aisles, Dr. Montrose said, "I'll need a stretcher."

"Already looking," came Munro's curt reply, irritated. Then, "Laddie buck, found one, come here."

Using the deceased policeman's handcuff keys, Munro freed Tucker's arm and leg from the two metal poles, then he and Lewis carefully slid his large body onto the stretcher. Lifting him up, they started back into the pitch darkness where their car was parked.

With Tucker's stretcher in the rear seat, Munro went back to turn off the supply room's lights and secure both rear doors. Three men in a cramped front seat, sounds of their breathing piercing the stillness.

"Mike, we killed a policeman."

"Ye been in a war, wee shite."

"Yeah, but this is America."

Dr. Montrose's cultured voice broke in, "Gentlemen, it's important," pointing toward the back seat, "that the police don't find this man and myself in your car."

"Aye, Doctor," Munro agreed. "A colored doctor and escaped prisoner in a sundown city might present a wee problem."

"Sundown city?" It was a term Lewis had never heard.

"We colored people aren't allowed in a white area after sundown," Dr. Montrose mused.

CHAPTER TWENTY-THREE

Physically and mentally exhausted, Lewis sped through Fort Lauderdale's blacked-out streets until Dr. Montrose's distinguished voice said, "Please, Mr. Blackthorne, slow down."

"The doctor's right, wee shite."

Cutting through residential neighborhoods, crossing the Seventh Avenue Bridge then stopping at a red light on Broward Boulevard. No streetlights or cars but too cautious to move through a red light. Finally green, they crossed into the safety of colored town.

"The storage room," Dr. Montrose said, "behind the Colored School."

A pause. Other than occasional forays to Sylvia Pinckney's Employment Agency, colored town was someplace he'd never been.

"Go to Northwest Fourth Street and Eleventh Avenue." Lewis detected the doctor's irritation. Fort Lauderdale had been laid out in a grid, but with numerous canals and rivers, maintaining a grid was difficult. But since few picturesque rivers ran through colored town, the grid was perfect.

The Colored School, where once a year dump trucks from the Broward County School Board backed up to offload used textbooks from white schools. Many with pages torn, others defaced by obscenities from white students who had used them.

Lewis was directed onto a bumpy open field where his bouncing headlights picked out people huddled near the school's north side.

Stopping, Dr. Montrose directed two men there to take Tucker's stretcher into a storage room. Fatigue, shock wearing off, Lewis's dazed mind realizing he'd just kidnapped Tucker from one storage room and delivered him to another one.

While the doctor stayed inside with his patient, the group gathered around Blackthorne and Munro. Almost blinded by Pastor Sims's flashlight in his face, Munro explained what happened. Then questions: "Why did Sheriff Parnell keep Martin Tucker alive? Why did you kill Sergeant Stark?"

Somewhere Lewis never imagined he'd ever be, with people considered inferior. *Am I a nigger-lover now?* Feeling a spring breeze sweep across the dark field, a sudden yearning to be near the ocean. Waves lapping onto a beach, the ocean's song.

Schoolteacher Estelle Claudel cut into his dreamlike state, her husky voice demanding, "Did Hampton Stark catch you there?"

"Catch us there, yes, Mrs. Claudel," Munro admitted. "We hadna' choice." A moan.

Quiet hung until Sylvia asked, "Mr. Lewis, will you be all right?"

Former enslaved, now segregated, people worried about someone white and privileged, Lewis felt both astonishment and guilt. "I'm fine, Sylvia, thank you." Still calling someone colored by their first name.

Seconds later Dr. Montrose left his patient in the storage room. "Mr. Tucker needs quiet; I'll keep a close eye on him."

Dawn found Munro and Lewis back on board the Shetlands, both savoring scotch's golden liquid burning down their throats. "We killed a cop, Mike."

Almost disinterested, Mike muttered, "Vast tub a' shite."

Scotland's liquid gift to the world was helping dull the night's madness. By their fourth drink both were slurring their words, "Be ready for Tuesday, ye wee shite."

A girlish giggle. "Oh, that? I'm...ready." Fatigue and anxiety from the night mixed with scotch. Drunk now, Lewis was desperate to close his eyes.

* * *

At near six that afternoon, groggy from assisting Mike through three bottles of scotch only hours before, Lewis slowly drove up Las Olas Boulevard to his office, receiving looks of concern from elevator operator David Lockhart.

Rhythmic bubbling from a coffee percolator then, cup in hand, Lewis stumbled toward his desk, a newspaper under his arm. Bleary eyes stared at bold headlines of the Fort Lauderdale Daily News: BELOVED POLICE SERGEANT MURDERED!

Grateful no suspects were named but a catch in his breath at finding no mention of the man chained up in the medical supply room. Martin Tucker didn't officially exist.

Then queasiness. Barely time to push the newspaper away before an ill-used stomach emptied its contents onto his desk. Feeling like death warmed over, he remembered another line from the movie *Casablanca*: "Round up the usual suspects." *Mike and I are the "usual suspects."*

This time he made it to the men's room. Kneeling over the porcelain throne on black and white dotted tiles, he realized that no amount of coffee courage could wash this away. Only one thing worse would be a phone call from Captain Harmon Drysdale in Port Everglades, announcing their game plan had moved up to right now.

Back in the office the phone did ring. Mally's loud voice asked, "Lewis, did you kill that policeman?"

He hesitated. "It's complicated."

"What do you mean complicated? Did you kill that policeman or not?"

Still slurring his words, he said, "Thought you were heading to Italy?"

"Lewis, have you been drinking?" No response. "My God, you're drunk."

"First off, I didn't kill anybody but thanks for your concern." Trying to stifle a burp, not succeeding then sounding cavalier. "Why aren't you at war?"

Profanity through the phone. “It was delayed—I’m leaving tomorrow. Tell me what happened.”

“Hold on a second.” He laid down the phone and scrambled to the coffee altar. A gulp of hot caffeine left his voice raspy. “Hampy Stark caught us getting Martin Tucker out.”

“Oh, my God.” Was she crying? “I interviewed the sheriff about Martin Tucker...Oh, my God, he must have panicked and sent them to the medical supply room. Where’s he now?”

“A safe place. For your information, Mally, they near beat him to death.”

He sensed her head nodding through the phone. “I’m not surprised.” Hot coffee collided with last night’s scotch sending the remnants of his stomach onto the desk. Again barely missing the headlines.

“You sound horrible, Lewis.”

There was a long silence, and then suddenly a whisper, “Lewis, I was molested by Uncle Dennis.” Stunned, Lewis heard her sobbing. “Eight years old, he gave me a disease. My mother blamed me, I was sent away.”

“That’s why you were always so different,” he said, barely audible. Different schools but living in the same neighborhood. Told that little girl down the street had rheumatic fever, was sent away to be treated.

“Mally, I love you.”

Soft muffled cries over the phone. “Please, Lewis, it’s too late now, my train leaves tonight...goodbye.” The phone disconnected.

CHAPTER TWENTY-FOUR

A vision suddenly gone. A roiling stomach forbade going back to the sailboat that night. He left his office and walked across a now traffic-free Andrews Avenue.

Entering the Broward Hotel, he was met by Artie Shaw's song "Begin the Beguine" wafting through the atrium. Sam Rothstein, his song. That song, understanding it for the first time, pain does that. That clarinet takes you up in the sky, opens your soul and explodes. Gently drifting down more alive. The song ended just as Lewis entered the elevator. On the second-floor hallway he stopped to knock on the door. *Why am I here?*

"Come in." Sarah Goldfine in a chair, a full slip over her knees, showing garter belt clips to her stockings, almost showing...

She knew I'd come.

Pretense gone, she was staring at him, wanting. "Where's your husband, Sarah?" *Her eyes, she's flirting.*

"Did you kill that policeman?"

Two women, same goddamn question. "I was there, but... no, I didn't kill him."

She waved him inside, no attempts at modesty. "Is there a connection between the death of my father and this policeman?"

"Probably... yes." *The way she's dressed.*

She stood up and walked over. "Jared's involved."

"Involved? Your husband, how?"

"When you started asking..." Flirting eyes dulled, grew sad.

"Weak, always been weak, hates me for knowing that. When we came back to our room I demanded to know what was going on. He finally admitted it. "

"Admitted what, Sarah?"

"That both he and Abba *had* approached those crime 'people' you were talking about. And took their front money, which means those people now own both of them. Jared thought he could play both sides. He can't. They forced him to give them information out of the District Attorney's Office, his own office."

Killing a policeman, the woman he'd loved gone. Then this...another Casablanca moment. Seeing her tears, vulnerability, Lewis embraced her. *Mally's gone, any port in a storm?* Warmth, desire being returned, something never felt before. Their lips together, a sensual wetness. Then: *Still the fuckin' altar boy.* He pulled back, awkward. "I'm sorry."

Her eyes, still wanting, sadly accepted. "She must be pretty special."

An involuntary nod. "Where's your husband now?"

The moment had passed. "He knew I'd never forgive him. He went to see the sheriff trying to play both sides. They scared him; he's gone."

CHAPTER TWENTY-FIVE

Ten the next morning. “Son, you look like you’re carrying the weight of the world on your shoulders,” the elevator operator said. Lewis patted the old man’s shoulder and left the elevator intent on a quiet walk downtown. Outside the Sweet Building he walked south on Andrews Avenue past the Sunset Theater.

Then the barber shop, old man Marshall cutting his hair for twenty-five cents every two weeks. Now by New River, seeing that most of the downtown charter fishing boats were miles offshore in the Gulf Stream.

Heavy traffic swarmed across the Andrews Avenue Bridge. *What Florida becomes after the war?* He gazed down at a swift outgoing tide winding its way eastward toward the ocean, entranced by black tidal water swirling around creosote coated pilings that supported the bridge. He spotted a tarpon roll. *New River, life hangs on.*

Warning bells and gates lowering, stopping cars so boat traffic could pass through. He’d read about complaints of clogged traffic on both Andrews Avenue and Federal Highway Bridge, the new Florida.

Turning away from gates and bells, heading back, this time on the east side of Andrews. The Deck Bar was open, crowded with sailors, even in the morning. South of the city, the Navy had taken over little-used Merle Fogg Airport, enlarging it to become Naval Air Station Fort Lauderdale. This and the Navy’s presence in Port Everglades meant many sailors on liberty in downtown

Fort Lauderdale. North past the newsstand, he found himself in front of the Broward Hotel, directly across from the Sweet Building where he started. Sarah.

A tall, impeccably dressed man approached, Willard Lancaster. *The man who killed my mother.*

CHAPTER TWENTY-SIX

If he'd thought Dennis Lancaster's office was plush, Willard's crept into the realm of exotic. The third floor, southeast corner of Las Olas and Andrews Avenue. Wood paneling surrounded two large windows with blue velvet curtains. Furniture consisted of Lancaster's hand-carved wooden chair and desk, supplemented by two plush chairs matching a dark brown leather couch.

Twinges of insecurity faded with Lewis's realization that this pompous display was a subconscious inducement to impress. "Care for a drink, Lewis?"

The man who killed my mother. Slow deep breaths, suppress. "No, thanks."

"Please sit down." Lewis noted intense brown eyes study him as Lancaster leaned forward, large cupped hands, long fingers dancing against each other's tips.

"I think it's time we talk."

Talk. The only time Willard Lancaster ever spoke to him was late April 1938 by St. Anthony's School, Lewis about to invite Mally to be his date at the prom.

Then that conversation: "Invite my daughter to the prom, your mother loses her job and will be blackballed with any law firm in town." Fighting to control emotions. *We wait, the war kinna' last forever."*

Unlike his brother, whose balding head sat over a fleshly face and pudgy body, Willard Lancaster was fit and handsome, even deep into his fifties. Thin, distinguished, well-cut straight gray hair crowned a sculpted face. Willard was everything his brother Dennis wasn't.

"Do you know what I think, Blackthorne?" Lancaster's wiry

body was coiled like a snake about to strike.

"Tell me what you think, Mr. Lancaster."

Surprised by that sophistication, the lawyer hesitated a moment. "I think you and that Scotsman are involved in the murder of our beloved police sergeant Hampton Stark."

Beloved police sergeant.

"Funny you should mention that, Mr. Lancaster. I was just wondering how you and Sheriff Walter Parnell figure into the murder of your former client Sam Rothstein... and Sylvia Pinckney's son Reuben." *Don't mention Mom. We wait, the war kinna' last forever.*

Lancaster's eyes blinked, a lifelong Florida tan drained from his face. "I've misjudged you, Lewis."

"I'll take that as a compliment, Mr. Lancaster." Lewis stood up to leave, "One question, Mr. Lancaster, what do you and those crime families in New York plan to do with your tracts of beachfront land after the war."

Recovering quickly, a good poker player, Lewis thought, as color returned to Lancaster's smooth olive-skinned face. Lewis hated skin like that, his own freckled cracker skin burned horribly. "You have to know this isn't going to end well for you, son."

Son? Murder my mother, not good enough to take your daughter to the senior prom, now son? At that moment a fresh breeze swept through both open windows. Lewis breathed in, mentally escaping to a seashore. "Breath of the ocean," his mother's words.

Pretense at civility disappeared. Getting up, Lancaster walked over and closed the door. "Sit down." Curious, Lewis obliged and sat back down. "As you've surmised, everything changes in Florida after the war—"

"I think your client Sam Rothstein's words were: Florida land is the new gold." Lewis smiled. "Why didn't you stop your brother Dennis from molesting Mally when she was a child? Her mother blamed her."

Hearing that, Lancaster's genteel façade disappeared, replaced by a sneer, a mental picture formed of someone breathing fire.

"She's gone, Mr. Lancaster."

"Gone? What are you talking about?"

"She left both of us, off to Europe, as a war correspondent."

The façade faded; his shoulders sagged. "I've badly misjudged you, Lewis. You might have had a future here with me after the war. As it is, I suspect your future is very much in doubt."

CHAPTER TWENTY-SEVEN

Wednesday, March 1, 1944

Just before closing, Henry Cole noticed something out of place on his desk. Drawers unlocked, he pulled the bottom one out and grabbed the precious manila envelope. It had been opened then sealed again, sloppily.

The rear door opened, employee William Arthur was leaving for the day, an instant calculation. Almost dark, most of the shops on Las Olas Boulevard had closed, leaving little pedestrian or vehicular traffic. "Bill, would you come back here, please?"

Seconds later William Arthur appeared at his office door, seeing the manila envelope in Cole's hands. "Yes, Mr. Cole?"

"Bill, my desk was unlocked—have you been in here?"

Panic in Arthur was compounded by Cole's more pronounced German accent. He stuttered, "I—I never go in your office, Mr. Cole, you know that." Then a careless caveat, "Unless of course it's something important."

"Why was it important for you to open this envelope, Bill?"

William Arthur's round face, even the tight gray curls on top of his head flowed with perspiration. "It—it—"

"Come here, Bill." Henry Cole got up, walked over to a file cabinet and pulled out a 9mm German Luger pistol. Arthur caught his breath. "Bill, who did you tell about this manila envelope?"

He'd loved the same woman since grade school, his child Charlie was a pride and joy… Arthur knew it had been a life well lived. "It's all in German, Mr. Cole," Arthur said calmly. "I have no goddamn idea what it said."

***

Later that evening, Deputy Sheriff Clyde Travis turned off his headlights then drove across the bumpy, sandspur-covered field to the Colored School. Night skies had cleared from rain showers moving through South Florida earlier in the evening, bringing soft, northeasterly breezes. A Florida winter's last dying gasp before summer's intense heat and humidity set in.

The engine off, he sat quietly, watching for any activity nearby. Emerging, flashlight in hand, he approached the portable storage building behind the school. A well-aimed kick near the door handle smashed through the jam, causing the door to fly open. Inside, his light beam found the empty mattress.

***

Sheriff Parnell never knew who Sergeant Stark's paid colored informant was; no one did. But after Stark was killed, Parnell told Clyde Travis that cash was no object in finding Martin Tucker. Money talks; information came.

What Sheriff Parnell didn't realize was that schoolteacher Estelle Claudel had *also* figured out who Hampton Stark's informant was. When she called her husband, Earnest Claudel, the informant disappeared.

***

Hearing footsteps in the cockpit that evening, Lewis and Munro rushed up to confront Estelle Claudel's husband. "Earnest, what is it?"

"Come quick, Cap'n Mike."

Following Claudel's old pickup into colored town, they returned an hour later with Martin Tucker. At dawn another visitor, this time a Navy enlisted man with an order: Meet Captain Harmon Drysdale at the Casino Pool, now.

CHAPTER TWENTY-EIGHT

Many of Lewis's fondest childhood memories occurred in the white stucco Mediterranean style enclosure known as the Casino Pool. Its entrance was guarded by a Spanish tower with wide front concrete steps that led down to a basketball court situated between the pool and the beach.

Saltwater pumped from the ocean into the Casino Pool began a three-day fill-and-empty process. Remembering goosebumps from jumping into the pool that first day it was refilled. Water temperature became bearable on the second day, and by day three its salt-and-chlorine water was so warm Lewis felt he was floating in a bathtub.

At closing on day three, the pool was drained, letting clear saltwater rush in from the ocean to mix with chlorine and begin the three-day process of cold, moderate and warm. Burning eyes, another distinct childhood memory from that mixture of saltwater and chlorine.

***

Captain Drysdale and Munro looked down on Lewis standing in the three-foot shallow end of the pool. The Navy captain's starched khaki uniform matching his personality, an impatient voice barked, "Okay, Blackthorne, nobody's here but us girls, give this equipment a good run-through." Lewis wanted to laugh at that, but seeing Drysdale's scowl and the Scotsman's usual brooding snarl he stayed silent.

"You're supposed to be the big goddamn underwater expert,

Blackthorne, see if it works!"

Munro handed the bulky contraption, with two large cylinders hidden under a hard metal cover, down to Lewis. Attached was a full face mask with small eye holes, the whole thing resembling a gasmask. The Lambertsen Lung was a self-contained oxygen breathing device. Militarily practical since no telltale bubbles were released to alert anyone on the surface.

Assisted by four lengths of corrugated breathing tubes and a one-way valve, pure oxygen inhaled from the right cylinder was transferred as carbon dioxide into the left cylinder. There, a CO2 filter scrubbed it clean before moving it to diving bags, one on each shoulder to be rebreathed. After enough oxygen had been metabolized, a demand value released supplemental oxygen from the right cylinder into the breathing bags.

From his own experience Lewis knew what the caveat was: you had to stay above twenty feet. Breathing pure oxygen much below that becomes poisonous. Often fatal. Munro bent down to assist Lewis into a cloth harness the equipment was attached to. Fins already on, Lewis pulled on his face mask and signaled Munro to turn on the oxygen.

Sliding underwater, sitting on the shallow pool bottom, alone, free from gravity and the complicated world above. Another escape.

Knowing an impatient Drysdale and Munro were waiting above, he rolled over face down and kicked his fins, beginning the journey to the twelve-foot deep end. Lewis had always wondered why it was OSS and not his own Navy that saw value in this equipment.

At the deep end Lewis adjusted weights he'd inserted into zipper pockets on the cloth jacket, just enough to give a slight negative buoyancy. When Lewis had asked about a rubber diving suit to protect him from cold ocean water, Drysdale refused, "Gulf Stream waters are warm." His first clue to where he was headed.

Buoyancy established, he already regretted the need to return to the world of air. Fins thrusting against the density of water, his equipment concern gave way to thoughts of Mally.

On the surface he stared into Drysdale's glowering face. "Spent enough goddamn time down there, Blackthorne? Can you pull it off?"

After pulling off his face mask, he said, "Sir, maybe if I knew what I'm supposed to pull off."

Grunts of disapproval from both men, then a command. "Monday, 1000 hours, you and Munro, in my office. Be there."

CHAPTER TWENTY-NINE

"Why am I here?" Martin Tucker asked, cramped inside the sailboat's galley.

Fatigue, too many long nights. "Son, ye might be a bit more grateful. 'Tweren't for the lad here, your chocolate arse'd still be chained up."

Tucker's hand stretched out to the Scotsman, an apology. "What happens now?"

A colored man speaking perfect English.

"Plan was t' sneak ye out at night to Miss Sylvia's friends in Palm Beach County. They were t' put you on a northbound train. But...things change."

Tucker sat back, reflecting. "What things changed?"

Someone on the cockpit deck.

Munro, finger to his lips, rushed up the ladder. Clyde Travis, alone, late at night just like with Andre LeFleur.

A night breeze flapped open his sport coat revealing a pistol the deputy Travis pulled out. "Get that nigger up here."

Munro's soft voice masked the desire for vengeance burning inside. "No colored man here, Deputy Travis. Search down there ye'self."

Alone, at night, Travis grew cautious. In an instant Munro's left hand chopped down onto Travis's wrist freeing the pistol, while his right fist snapped the deputy's head back, causing him to fall backward. Munro immediately dropped, knees digging deep into Travis's stomach. Dazed, out of breath.

Hearing the commotion, Lewis started for the ladder but was pushed aside. Martin Tucker leaped past him, thrusting a knife no one knew he had, deep into the deputy's chest. A team, Munro and Tucker pinned a bleeding Travis down while Munro's hand suppressed any cries of alarm.

Lewis made it on deck in time to watch Clyde Travis's life and blood drain away. Munro stood up and spat down on the body. Again cursing out, "Tis for Martha, tis for Andre LeFleur."

Another policeman dead.

All three men anxiously scanned the night, deathly quiet, feeling fresh breezes playing across the black waters of Las Olas Sound. Then Tucker collapsed. Beatings, concussion, energy spent.

"Help me, laddie buck, let's get him below."

Securing Tucker in a forward cabin, Lewis scampered up the ladder to recover the dead man's car keys as Munro stayed below searching for scotch. "Mike, help me get…this to its car."

Topside, bottle in hand, Munro stared at him. "Lad—?"

"Mike, follow me in your car, we'll drive up Las Olas to an island they haven't developed yet. Back in the mangroves…they won't find him for days."

"Quick thinkin', wee shite."

CHAPTER THIRTY

Ten p.m. Tuesday, March 7, 1944

The plans William Arthur copied stipulated the exact time and location that Henry Cole was to intercept the German U-boat. Three hours earlier, Lewis and Munro positioned themselves nearby. Heavy seas, no moon with thick fluffy clouds scudding over them. It was cramped in the small Navy-issued boat because Martin Tucker refused to stay behind.

"Mike, listen...no lights, a boat!"

Munro pulled the cord to his Johnson 25-horsepower kicker and cautiously followed the sound. Ten minutes later Cole's skiff was tied up alongside a Type IX C German U-boat. Lewis stripped down to a bathing suit, donned his gear and quietly slipped over the side, down to a depth of six feet.

Always amazed by visibility at night underwater, he started north, his eyes glued to the luminous compass dial. Assisted by the Gulf Stream's strong north-running current, in four minutes he was underneath the submarine's dark hull.

Then a problem. Maintaining proper buoyancy at this depth was difficult since heavy seas kept thrusting the U-boat up only to slam it right back down, narrowly missing his head. Feeling his way under the hull to the U-boat's starboard mid-section, he found the point where Cole's boat and the submarine were tied together.

Above him, both boats continually smacked against each other as six darkly clad men and equipment awkwardly moved from the submarine's pitching deck onto Kohler's even more unstable twenty-foot open boat.

Desperate to keep from being squashed between the crafts,

Lewis unstrapped the limpet mine from his waist and clamped it to the submarine's metal hull. Powerful magnets within the mine kept it attached to anything metal—the limpet mine was named after a sea snail of the same name which clings to rocks.

Device attached, Lewis dropped down to a ten-foot depth and started swimming north, desperate to increase the distance between himself and his prey. Moments later, a lookout topside on the U-boat heard Munro's engine. Automatic fire erupted with two rounds finding Munro's side and leg. Before falling over he turned the kicker's handle sending the small boat seaward.

Just as men and equipment finished transferring onto Cole's boat, four-and-a-half pounds of explosives inside the limpet mine ignited, destroying Cole's boat and occupants. The mine's impact also punctured the sub's pressure hull, igniting its torpedoes. Shafts of bright red and yellow fire screamed into a night sky.

Thanks to his fins and the Gulf Stream, Lewis had managed to be a good distance away, but shock from the explosions underwater still almost punctured his eardrums. The plan was for Lewis to surface at the prescribed time, then wait on the surface. Munro was to circle back to the proper longitude, proceed north and find him.

Surfacing at the specified time, Lewis was met by rising seas and sights of fiery flotsam floating off to his south. When the flotsam sank, Lewis was left alone in the darkness with no signs of Munro.

Water temperature in the Gulf Stream is decidedly warmer than the ocean's. But with no protective rubber suit and adrenalin wearing off, Lewis's body began to rapidly cool. Then with fatigue, it was becoming difficult to remain on the surface. Heavy with gear, his body was imploring relief in the depths.

Cold, energy depleting by the second, he remembered his OSS and UDT training: water 800 times denser than air means body heat is stripped away twenty-five times faster. Harder now to stay on the surface, legs starting to cramp. Deep in ocean troughs, panic creeping closer. Minutes went by, then an hour. Delusional with searing pain from leg cramps and barely conscious, he didn't see or hear Munro's boat coming alongside. Nor did his mind comprehend the powerful black arms reaching down, pulling him back onboard a rocking boat. Caught between hypothermia and delusion, Lewis called out for the Scotsman.

An educated voice responded, "They opened fire, I am afraid your friend has been shot."

"Who are you?"

"I'm the black man who saved your cracker ass."

Mind slowly clearing, Lewis recognized the voice.

"I'm sorry, it took me some time to stop his bleeding. Your friend needs a doctor."

Pitch dark, detecting Munro's huge form and a colored person speaking perfect English. "You? How'd you find me?"

"The compass, Mr. Blackthorne. Before passing out, your friend kept screaming for me to find the burning wreckage then keep the compass at zero degrees due north." While talking, Tucker removed Lewis's gear, replacing it with a shirt and pants. Helpless, a child. Even wrapping him in a blanket with gulps of hot coffee Munro had insisted on bringing. Warmth, semblance of rational thought returning.

He stared at the colored man, incredulous. "You found me out here?"

Mike Munro's deep raspy voice came from the bow. "Wee shite, are ye okay?" Happy hearing Munro's voice, and extremely grateful people other than white were intelligent and functional.

"Thank you...Martin Tucker."

"I figure this makes us even, Mr. Blackthorne," Tucker said, moving the kicker's handle around to guide their small boat toward Port Everglades.

CHAPTER THIRTY-ONE

Just past four in the morning found Mally Lancaster waiting in darkness as the boat beached onto the island's south side. Mally's flashlight temporarily blinded Lewis when he stepped off into several inches of brackish water.

His first steps on land started his legs cramping again. Pain, then the shock of seeing her. "Lewis, I've found your mother's journal!"

Not comprehending, "Her journal?"

Tucker almost knocked him over assisting Munro off the boat where he collapsed on a small grass and rock area. Before passing out he looked up at Mally, "Lad, this be yer split-tail?"

Out of the darkness came another shock, Dr. Kamau Montrose. "Mally, you brought a colored—"

"Yes, she brought a colored doctor," Dr. Montrose said matter-of-factly, kneeling over Munro.

Mally, flush with excitement, said, "Jack O'Hara got to Georgia and found Helen Tindall and the journal...it's all in there." She was trembling. "I never accepted that cockamamie story of yours, suddenly showing up as a private detective. Then tonight, those explosions offshore, I contacted Sylvia. She knew about tonight and—"

"Sylvia knew?"

Mally dismissed that. "She and your Scotsman go back a long way—thank God she trusted me. Explosions tonight...worried there'd be casualties. Sylvia agreed and contacted Dr. Montrose."

Leaving a dazed Lewis, she walked over and asked, "How is he, Dr. Montrose?"

"Martin was able to stop the bleeding." The doctor stood up, facing a wobbling Tucker. His eyes rolled back, beginning the journey to unconsciousness. Lewis recovered enough to help ease Tucker down next to Munro. "Both men need a hospital. Miss Mally, would you please drive us over to Provident Hospital?"

Lewis protested, "Provident Hospital's in colored town, she can't—"

"Take two colored men to a colored hospital?" the doctor laughed, "Yes, Mr. Blackthorne, a white woman taking two *colored* men anywhere in the middle of the night would not look good in Fort Lauderdale."

An exhausted mind trying to reason out madness in the middle of the night. "Mally, get on Mike's boat over there—I'll be right back."

On some level relieved to see the dreamer so assertive, she conceded but with a question, "Lewis, what is a split-tail?"

CHAPTER THIRTY-TWO

Dawn was breaking when Lewis stepped back onboard, seeing bloodstains missed from a wash-down two nights ago. Below deck Mally handed him a cup of coffee. "How are they?"

He took a sip. "Fine I guess. Dr. Montrose says Mike and Tucker are safe for now...at least until some paid informant runs to tell the sheriff."

Nervous about the bloodstains, caffeine pushing back fatigue. "Thought you were leaving?"

"Something came up." She smiled. "You."

Events started to collate in his mind. "Mom's journal?"

She took it out of her purse, sat on the cushion and handed it to him. "Yesterday I went up to my father's office to confront him—"

"Confront? What about?"

"Uncle Dennis. What he'd done to me as a child, the scars inside... Father and I had never discussed it."

"Well, I mentioned it to him."

She gasped. "Did he know?"

"He knew."

Her eyes full of questions welled up.

"Yeah, invited me to his office, curious about what I was up to. When he threatened me I just threw it out there, about you... and Uncle Dennis."

She asked again, still hoping, "He knew?"

"I'm sorry, Mally, you could read it in his face, yeah, he knew."

Pain, her head down, crying, he opened the journal... where to begin. She broke into his search. "I went to confront my father but ran into Jack O'Hara. I'd forgotten, the man barely walks, even with a—"

"I know, I know, it's sad." He was sympathetic but was impatient to know about the journal. "Jack gave you Mom's journal? You, the daughter of Willard Lancaster?"

"He asked me to step inside his office…then shut the door."

"Then what happened?"

"Jack sort of stalled around, asked if I'd seen you. All the time keeping his eye on the door." She paused. "You need to understand something, Lewis. Confronting my father would be a life-altering moment."

Impatient, wanting to read the journal but stifling impulses. "Sorry, can't imagine how difficult—"

"But seeing Jack's manner, it just poured out. I babbled on God knows how long, but he listened. The next thing I know the journal is on his desk."

"Why not give it to me himself?"

"He's gone, resigned from the firm, was leaving for Boston—some contacts from Harvard offered him a position."

Everything happening at once. "Did you read it?"

Her voice broke. "We both read it. My God, your mother was meticulous, she'd been documenting things for years."

"Like what?"

"That beachfront land, my father's plans—"

"Gambling casinos?"

"How did you know about that?" Again astonished at the dreamer.

"Those were Sam Rothstein's visions…before your father murdered him, his own client." *Florida land, the new gold.*

Sam Rothstein was a rabbit hole she didn't want to go down. Instead, she said, "Your mom used a term in her journal I'd never heard before: 'crime families'?"

"Organized crime families, the mob. Rothstein explained it all to me."

"And I'm supposed to be the reporter." She smiled. "Your mother described how two of those *crime families* were using my father's firm to buy off state legislators so they'd enact legislation to allow gambling casinos in South Florida."

"The land was for casinos, right on Fort Lauderdale's beach?"

"That was their plan. On the beach with elegant hotels. Sun, seas and the best food in the world. It's all there in the journal. They meant for Fort Lauderdale to become the gambling mecca of America!"

Putting pieces together. "That's why they killed Sam Rothstein—his dream wasn't in their plans."

"That's not all, Lewis. Your mom explained how the crux of it was getting money to build those two bridges that connected Tenth Street to the beach."

"Where'd that money come from?"

"Federal money—it's called pork. Congressmen insert funding money into other bills ready to sign."

Fort Lauderdale, gambling mecca of America. Her father, my mother's killer.

"That day, did you confront your father about Uncle Dennis?"

"After reading that journal, I couldn't, too...it was devastating." She refilled her cup. "Lewis, what is a split-tail? Why did that vulgar Scottish man say I was your split-tail?"

His answer was barely audible. "It's a Southern expression, Mally. A rather crude one I'm afraid."

"What's it mean?"

He felt everything he'd been through tonight was going to be easier than this. "Christ, really, you want to go into that, now?"

Not moving, green eyes boring through him, he sighed. Again barely audible, he muttered, "It denotes a woman's...vagina. You know how it's sort of split—"

"Okay, okay, I get it... I have one." Embarrassed, a nervous laugh. "You men are really stupid sometimes."

"Guilty." Blue eyes flirting with green eyes. "Look, Mally, I'm happy you're here."

"You are?" She hardly got that out before his lips met her

mouth. Unleashed passion, tasting, gentle biting. Grappling together they fell back on the cushion as cups with coffee dropped onto the deck.

Not here.

He stood up, gently pulling her forward, no resistance. On his bunk, their hands exploring, her soft moans with rapid warm breaths washing across his face as clothes came off. *Not like that whorehouse in Manila. Life's real meaning.*

When he pulled a blanket over their naked bodies later, she asked, "Lewis, the Navy brought you back here, to do this...thing you did tonight. Why didn't they at least help? And why didn't you take that vulgar man from Scotland to their facilities in the port?"

Spent, past exhaustion, he yawned. "Jesus, are you ever not a reporter?"

Her hand moved under the blanket, stopping between his legs. "For the past ten minutes I didn't think I was."

Naked, rolling off the bunk he headed aft to the galley, to Mike's scotch. Another shock was watching her snatch a glass from his hand and gulp it straight down. *The girl I had banana splits with at Beck's Drug Store.* Slowly savoring his own single malt, yawning, he was desperate to close his eyes. Not yet.

"Mally, none of this can get into the newspaper."

Someone else searching for sleep. "It's not getting in the paper, but tell me why the Navy, your Navy, didn't help you."

Searching her face, wanting to believe. "I mean it, Mally."

Too tired to answer, a simple nod. "Just tell me why the Navy didn't do this."

"Okay, from the start I was told this had to stay secret. My Navy contact, Captain Drysdale, had a relationship with Mike Munro—"

"That vulgar man from Scotland?"

Weary of hearing that, he said, "Yes, that vulgar man from Scotland. Anyway, Mike and Captain Drysdale go back to World War I, two young officers from different navies. After the war Mike became part of a British secret intelligence service called MI6."

Hesitation. *A bootlegger working for MI6?* Then Lewis remembered the Bahamas belonged to the Britain.

"What is it?"

"Nothing. After MI6 decoded information about a possible attack on Port Everglades, they used Mike's relationship with Captain Drysdale, had him act as a go-between."

"Go-between? Why?"

"Because the Navy and our new intelligence service, the OSS, don't like each other. Politics. MI6 understood all this but needed Captain Drysdale and his Navy to work with the OSS, sort of off the books. When Captain Drysdale confirmed that British intelligence was right about Port Everglades, I was brought back from the Pacific."

He paused. "A good friend was murdered getting that confirmation. By the same German bastard driving that boat out there tonight. I...he's gone now."

"And you never told me, you, my sensitive dreamer."

"They'd shoot me for telling you this."

Snuggling closer, a giggle. "Another secret I have to sleep with." She frowned. "Hell of a story, though."

She must have noticed his worried expression. "Look, Sylvia trusted me—you can too." Her mind always working, she added, "What else haven't you told me, Lewis?"

Why not? "Clyde Travis showed up here two nights ago looking for Martin Tucker—"

"You killed that deputy sheriff, too?"

"I didn't kill him."

"You keep saying that. A dead policeman in the hospital. Now this, another one?" His nod confirmed that, as she listened to him describe dumping Travis's car and body on a mangrove island off Las Olas. A noise on deck, more than one person.

CHAPTER THIRTY-THREE

Captain Drysdale with two enlisted men confronted Lewis in the cockpit. "Blackthorne, where's our boat?" Seeing Mally, he said, "Who are you?"

A mock curtsy from Mally as Lewis introduced her to Captain Harmon Drysdale. "You're *that* reporter?"

That reporter? "I am, yes."

"Blackthorne, what's she know?"

"Pretty much everything," Lewis admitted. "You can trust her."

"Trust a reporter?" Drysdale's wrath was about to descend on Lewis when he saw Mally tuck in Lewis's shirt. Domesticity. "Are you two married?"

He was glad for the reprieve. "Not married...yet."

Remembering his two enlisted men next to him, Drysdale turned. "Mullins here is a coxswain, came to get our boat back to the port. Where is it?"

"Beached across the street, sir."

"Mullins, you and your mate get that boat back onto Navy property, now."

"Aye, aye, sir." The coxswain saluted, knowing this was about desire for privacy. A curt nod from Mullins and both men disappeared.

"I just learned that you got yourself involved in colored town again. You and Munro killed some policeman...and kidnapped a colored prisoner?"

"Actually, two policemen are dead now," Lewis admitted, his voice low.

"Two cops…dead! Is Mike a part of this?"

Waves of fatigue, desperate for sleep. "It's complicated, but yes, sir, we're both involved."

The captain's expression was apoplectic. "Blackthorne, I'm here to fight a goddamn world war, you know, defeat the enemy. Not this…two cops dead?"

"Two policemen dead," Lewis conceded again.

Captain Drysdale's face contorted, a pause, then, "Tell me straight, son, did you do anything wrong here? I mean wrong morally?"

"No, Captain Drysdale," Mally injected, "all Lewis did was help innocent people. That man he 'kidnapped' saved Lewis and that vulgar Scotsman."

Starched personality melted. "Quite a spitfire you got there." A deep breath. "Your record, Blackthorne, what you accomplished last night…where's Mike?"

"He was injured, shot last night, Captain."

"Shot, is he okay, where is he?"

"A colored hospital."

"A colored hospital? Why not bring him to our medical facilities in the port?"

"My question exactly," Mally interrupted.

Her temerity gave Lewis courage. "You demanded secrecy, sir. Said nothing comes back on the Navy. Told me we're on our own, sir."

Drysdale nodded, shamed. "I didn't want it that way, son. The Chief of Naval Operations, Admiral King, hates MI6 and OSS. He would have killed the whole thing." Now Lewis heard a fatherly tone. "I'll get our people, we'll get Mike back to Port Everglades—"

"But that colored man, sir. He saved us; the sheriff finds him…he's dead."

Drysdale's face started to contort again, then a sigh. "Okay, we'll get both of them to our doctors." He glanced at Mally. "Marry this girl, Blackthorne, you're a damn fool if you don't."

"I will, sir, but...what about Mike's sailboat? Eventually that bread crumb trail leads back here...to Mike and me."

Drysdale cocked his head. "Bread crumb trail? Not satisfied at being a goddamn private eye, now you're fuckin' poet too?" Shaking his head, smiling. "Believe it or not, some of us in this man's Navy can still actually sail a boat. Can you sail, Blackthorne?"

"Mike took the Shetlands out at least once a week, he made a real sailor out of me."

"Good, my exec sails too. We'll be back in an hour. With this northeast wind the three of us will sneak Mike's boat into Port Everglades before dark."

When they were alone Mally asked, "Lewis, did you just propose marriage to me?"

Those teasing green eyes, he kissed her hand. "Yes. We have an hour before he gets back, Mally."

CHAPTER THIRTY-FOUR

December 1945

Memories, so much had happened. A brutal winter crossing, glad to see the little island again. Tying up the Shetlands, he headed to the bridge tender shack. Old Hoke, manning the two-lane wooden swing bridge, Fort Lauderdale's first connection to the beach. Elated, time gone by, a warm welcome, asking to use Hoke's 1936 Ford coupe.

It was a mild December afternoon as the Scotsman drove past those stately royal palm trees on Las Olas Boulevard toward downtown. Past Maus and Hauffman's men's store, a dress shop and the Horizon Bar. That damn red light at Federal Highway.

Seeing the Pioneer House Restaurant at the foot of the Federal Highway Bridge, traffic backed well north of Lauderdale High. Waiting, seeing Firestone Tire Store busy now those wartime restrictions had been lifted.

Bridge down, green light, moving west on Las Olas Boulevard. Colony Theatre, Beck's Drug Store and Fannin Funeral Home to the Governor's Club Hotel on First Avenue. Amazed that sailors were still lined up outside the Florida Theater. Blount Building, Stag and Doe bar, then stopping at Andrews Avenue.

He looked up to the third floor of the Broward National Bank Building. The reason he came back.

Turning right on Andrews, past the Tropical Arcade, Maryland Hotel, City Hall and the Sears, Roebuck and Company store. Across from Sears was the Union Bus Station, terminal for Greyhound and city buses. War over, yet military uniforms still jamming both bus stations.

Stopping at Broward Boulevard, happy to see the Woman's Club still tucked inside Stranahan Park. Two blocks north then west on Northwest Second Street. Across railroad tracks, past City Ice and Fuel Plant to Sylvia Pinckney's Employment Agency. Munro walked across dirt that went for a front yard onto concrete blocks that went for front steps. Seconds later a scream, "Cap'n Mike!"

Powerful arms wrapped the old colored woman in a bear hug. "Miss Sylvia." Her smile quickly erased by sadness.

"Mr. Lewis, he's dead."

"I know, Miss Sylvia. Last December, a kamikaze plane struck his ship off Okinawa. I was in England but Captain Drysdale made sure to notify me."

She moaned, "And Miss Mally, she dead too?"

Hearing that, the Scotsman lowered his head. "Yes, Miss Sylvia. The first American journalist gutsy and savvy enough to get into Berlin." He cursed softly. "Two days before the war ended, a sniper got her…barely a boy."

Tears from both as they embraced, Munro's voice breaking. "The lass and lad are gone." Remembering a hurried wedding performed by Captain Drysdale. That blissful week spent hiding from the police inside Port Everglades before Lewis was shipped back to the Pacific. Moments of happiness. Finding the right one, so rare in life.

Then, "There was a child, Miss Sylvia."

The old woman gasped. "A baby? Mr. Lewis and Miss Mally, a baby?" Shock clouded sadness.

"Aye, a wee lass, Kathleen." He wiped tears. "Born in England where Mally was a correspondent. Two days later Lewis was reported killed."

Her face was anguished. "But the baby? Who taking—"

This was going to be difficult. "Mally learned that Lewis's fifth grade teacher, Sister Catherine Patricia, had returned to Ireland before the war."

Sylvia persisted, "What about the baby?"

He needed to get through this. "The nun he loved, taught him the Latin responses to serve mass. Even sneaking wee Lewis onto an altar to practice where no women were allowed to be."

"But, Cap'n Mike, the baby?"

"After Lewis's death, Mally was desperate to get back to the front line and finish...finish the war for Lewis."

Sylvia's expression, waiting for an answer. "Mally left three-month-old Kathleen with Sister Catherine Patricia in Dublin, in a Dominican convent."

"Who will raise the child, who will—"

"I will raise the child when I finish my business here, Miss Sylvia."

A suspicious look. "What business, Cap'n Mike? Da sheriff and police is still lookin' for you and Mr. Lewis. Dey know'd you and Mr. Lewis killed dem policemen."

Gentleness disappeared. Small brown eyes stared through slits above a high cheek-boned face. Stone cold, someone Sylvia had never seen.

Understanding this, Munro reverted back to that other self, as each took a moment, adjusting to the reality of post-war America. "Tell me, Miss Sylvia, your work, getting people registered to vote."

"Dat sheriff, he worse now, Cap'n Mike. Ain't gonna be no votin' for us, people's gone scared."

"I see."

This was to be butcher and bolt. Skills honed the past two years of war that he spent with Special Operations Executive. SOE, Winston Churchill's invention, designed to set Europe ablaze. No intelligence-gathering organization like MI6, this was tactical, in the field, killing. Begrudgingly, at Churchill's insistence, MI6 had reassigned the Scotsman to SOE. Two years of killing. This was to be butcher and bolt, a vengeance raid.

But a hesitation, wondering which battle to fight now, which battle to leave for another day? "And yer nephew, Martin?"

That made her smile. "Dat boy's safe up North in law school.

Mr. Thurgood Marshall hisself wants Martin to join him in the NAACP." A few minutes more of conversation, expressions of hope for the future.

One more stop, a visit to Lewis's friend, elevator operator David Lockhart. Small-town gossip overheard, Lancaster's wife visiting family in Georgia, not due back until tomorrow.

Just past midnight, Munro parked Hoke's Ford close to the two-story stucco white house on the south side of Himmarshee Canal. Current home of Willard Lancaster from the law firm of Lancaster, Lancaster, Hardwicke and Chandler.

Bedroom pitch black, a light switched on. With a knife at his throat, Lancaster looked up into the cruel brown eyes of Black Mike Munro.

Deep voice, unmistakable brogue, "Ye killed Martha Blackthorne." Recognition, knife point not quite breaking skin on a throat, eyes searching for escape.

"Where's yer brother?"

The blade eased back. Lancaster gasped, "Dennis shot himself last year. What do you want?"

"You, noble barrister, you and yer filthy brother, the bastard who molested yer daughter."

Hiding acknowledgement of that, getting a breath, thinking, the man said, "My wife's due back any moment, you'd better leave."

"Know ye have a granddaughter, barrister? And with Lewis, the lad ye hated so much." No hiding rage now but still searching for a way. Suddenly the Scotsman paused on his vengeance raid. Older, weary, another war with so many killed.

Sensing hesitation, Lancaster moved. Too late. Munro's blade already deep into the lawyer's throat. Gurgling, blood spurting on sheets, splashing up onto Munro. Thrashing but held down by powerful arms.

Then still.

In the dark of night two hours later, the forty-two-foot ketch Shetlands sailed out into the Atlantic Ocean, tacking off strong northeast winds, its mainsail reefed in wild December seas.

The Bahamas, then making for Africa, slowly clawing north to Dublin, to wee Kathleen. Then Scotland.

The Scotsman would never see tomorrow's headlines from Fort Lauderdale Daily News: PROMINENT LOCAL ATTORNEY FOUND MURDERED IN BED.

Smaller print underneath: "Sheriff Walter Parnell assumes full control of investigation." Near the bottom of page one: "North Florida legislators, known here as the 'Pork Chop Gang,' override South Florida legislators in their attempt to introduce gambling casinos in Florida." A caveat: horse and dog racing would, however, continue.

Few in town would bother reading the article hidden on page five: "Dateline Las Vegas. New gambling casinos open on Fremont Street. Mayor Ernie W. Cragin's office announces that Las Vegas will become the gambling mecca of America."

Made in the USA
Columbia, SC
12 November 2021